"You're hopelessly distrustful."

Suddenly the defiance left her expression. Rory wished he would have had time to get ready for what she did next. Grace laid her hand on his wrist.

Everything she was was in that touch. The way she was dressed tried to say one thing about her: that she was a polished and successful businesswoman. But her touch said something entirely different. That she was gentle, a little naïve, hopeful about life. She was too soft and too gullible. He was not sure how she had managed to remain that way through life's tragedies—the death of her brother, the break-up of her engagement. There was a kind of courage in it that he reluctantly admired even while he felt honor-bound to discourage it.

He both admired her hope and wanted to kill it before it did some serious damage.

Grace turned and looked at Rory, those amazing eyes dancing with the most beautiful light. And the light in her eyes was doing the strangest thing to him. Grace's light was piercing the darkness in him, bringing brightness to a place that had not seen it for a long, long time.

He did not allow himself to marvel at it. He thrust the feeling of warmth away. His darkness could put out her light in a millisecond. And he'd better remember that when he was thinking about how beautiful Graham's kid sister had become.

Dear Reader

I've just had another perfect summer. I had the opportunity to do plenty of swimming in two of the world's most wonderful lakes: Lake Pend O'reille in Idaho, and Kootenay Lake in BC, in Canada. I also had lots of company this summer, ate ice cream, drank iced cappuccinos and sat in the shade just contemplating life.

And while I was having this fantastic, carefree summer so many young men and women who have answered the call to protect their nations were so far from home.

I write about soldiers because I have always thought it takes a special kind of courage to leave all the comforts (that I generally take for granted) behind. I am aware that the peace and prosperity I enjoy are ultimately linked to a young stranger's willingness to serve and to sacrifice.

So this one is dedicated to them, with heartfelt gratitude.

Cara Colter

BATTLE FOR THE SOLDIER'S HEART

BY
CARA COLTER

First published in Great Britain 2010
by Mills & Boon, an imprint of Harlequin (UK) Limited,
Eton House, 18-24 Paradise Road, Richmond, Surrey TW9 1SR

© Cara Colter 2012

ISBN: 978 0 263 22740 6

Cara Colter lives on an acreage in British Columbia with her partner Rob and eleven horses. She has three grown children and a grandson. She is a recent recipient of the *RT Book Reviews* Career Achievement Award in the Love and Laughter category. Cara loves to hear from readers, and you can contact her or learn more about her through her website, www.cara-colter.com

Recent books by Cara Colter:

THE COP, THE PUPPY AND ME
TO DANCE WITH A PRINCE
RESCUED BY HIS CHRISTMAS ANGEL
WINNING A GROOM IN 10 DATES
RESCUED IN A WEDDING DRESS

Did you know these are also available as eBooks?
Visit www.millsandboon.co.uk

To all the men and women who serve,
with deepest gratitude.

CHAPTER ONE

THERE were Shetland ponies everywhere.

They were gobbling the long strands of grass that sprouted around the brightly painted legs of the children's playground equipment. They were chowing down on the weeping-willow fronds at the edge of the duck pond.

Three had found their way through the chain-link fence and were grazing with voracious appetite on the green temptations of the Mason Memorial Soccer Field.

One had its face buried in the remnants of a birthday cake, and another, wandering toward the wading pool, was trailing a banner that said Happy Birthday, Wilson Schmelski.

From where he stood at the pedestrian bridge that crossed into the city of Mason's most favored civic park, Pondview, Rory Adams counted eight ponies on the loose.

And only one person trying to catch them.

"You little monster! You beady-eyed ingrate!"

The woman lunged right, the pony left.

If it had been anyone else, he might have allowed himself to see the humor in her predicament.

Instead, he frowned. When he thought of Gracie Day,

somehow, even after speaking to her on the phone, he hadn't factored in the passage of time. She was frozen in his mind at fourteen or fifteen. All glittering braces and freckles, skinned knees, smart-alecky and annoying.

To him, six years her senior, Gracie, his best friend's little sister, had not even been a blip on his radar. He had not considered her a *girl* in the sense that he considered girls. And at that age? Had he ever considered anything but girls?

He'd been twenty-one when he saw her last. He and Graham mustering out, on their first tour of Afghanistan, and her looking at him with fury glittering in her tear-filled eyes. *I hate you. How could you talk him into this?*

Graham had started to argue—the whole let's-go-play-soldier thing had been his idea, after all—but Rory had nudged him, and Graham had understood instantly.

Let me take it, let me be the bad guy in your kid sister's eyes.

The memory made him wince. They had looked out for each other. They'd had each other's backs. Probably thousands of times since they had said good-bye to Gracie that day. But the one time it had really counted...

Rory shook off the thoughts, and focused on the woman chasing ponies.

That *kid* sister.

Gracie Day was small and slender, deliciously curved in all the right places. Auburn hair that had probably started the day perfectly controlled and prettily coiffed, had long since surrendered to humidity and the pitfalls of pony-chasing. Her hair was practically hissing with bad temper and fell in a wild wave to her bare sun-kissed shoulders.

She was daintily dressed in a wide-skirted cream sundress and matching heels that had probably been perfect for the children's birthday party her event-planning company had just hosted.

But if Gracie had worked at it, she couldn't have chosen a worse outfit for chasing ponies.

The dress was looking rumpled, one slender strap kept sliding off her shoulder, and not only couldn't she get up any speed in those shoes, but the heels kept turning in the grass. At first glance, the smudge on the delectable rise of her bosom might have been mistaken for part of the pattern on the dress. But a closer look—that was *not* the bosom she'd had at fourteen—and he was pretty sure the bright-green splotch was horse slobber.

"Do you have any idea what glue is made from? Do you?"

Something still in her, then, of that fourteen-year-old girl she had once been. That girl was closer to the surface than the cool, calm and collected Gracie Day she had managed to convince him she was when he had spoken to her on the phone.

"I need to talk to you," he'd said, when he'd finally made it home. By then Graham had already been gone for six months. He'd wanted to tell her the truth.

I failed.

"I can't see why we would need to talk," she'd responded, and the fact was, he'd been relieved.

Talking about what had happened to Graham—and his part in it—was not going to be easy. And while he was not a man who shirked hard things, he had been thankful for the reprieve.

Rory felt a shiver along his spine. They said it was

survivor's guilt, but in his heart he felt it *was* his fault her brother hadn't come home.

Somehow, instead of being a temporary diversion, playing soldier had turned into a career for both of them. Graham, on their third deployment, Afghanistan again, had taken a bullet.

Rory still woke almost every night, sweating, his heart pounding.

Two teenage boys. Something about them. He'd hesitated because they were so young. And then bullets everywhere. Ducking, taking cover. Where was Graham? Out there. Crawling out, pulling him back, cradling him in his arms.

Blood, so much blood.

But the dream woke him before it was done. There was a piece missing from it, words he could not remember though he chased after them once he was awake.

The dream never told him what he needed to know. Had it been those boys? Were they the ones who had fired those shots? What could he have done differently? Could he have shoved Graham behind him, taken it instead?

Check up on Gracie. Those words whispered, a plea.

You didn't take a dying request lightly. And especially not the dying request of the man who'd been his best friend for more than ten years.

So, back home for six months now, Rory had tried. He called Gracie twice, and admittedly had been somewhat relieved to have been coolly rejected each time. The dreams were bad enough without the reality of having to tell her what had happened, while at the same time sparing her what had happened.

And so, he had followed the letter of Graham's instruction and checked up on her. While he had been away, the company he and his own brother had started—they had begun with race-car graphics and were now taking on the world—had succeeded beyond his wildest dreams. Once home, done with the military for good, Rory Adams was amazed to find himself a man with considerable resources.

One of whom was named Bridey O'Mitchell. Officially, she was his personal assistant. Unofficially, he considered her his secret weapon.

Bridey, middle-age, British, unflappable, could accomplish anything. Some days, Rory entertained himself by finding impossible challenges for her.

Can you get ice cream delivered to that crew working on the graphics for those Saudi airplanes? I know it's short notice, but do you think you could find half a dozen tickets to the sold-out hockey game? I'd like a koala bear and two kangaroos at the opening of that Aussie tour company we did the buses for.

Checking up on Gracie Day? That had been child's play for Bridey.

And the ensuing report about Gracie Day had been soothingly dull. Gracie was no longer engaged to the fiancé Graham had disliked intensely, and she ran a successful event-planning company, Day of Your Life, here in Mason, in the Okanagan Valley of British Columbia. Hers was the "it" company for weddings and anniversaries and special events.

The company had just been chosen to do the major annual fundraiser for Warrior Down, the organization that helped wounded vets and their families.

But Gracie's bread and butter was birthday parties for the children of the well-heeled, politicians and doctors and lawyers and CEOs. She put together the kind of parties that had clowns in them. And bouncy tents. Maybe a magician. And fireworks. The ponies must be an added touch since Rory had received Bridey's very thorough report.

Gracie Day organized the kind of parties that he had never had. In fact, he didn't recall his birthday ever being celebrated, except on one memorable occasion when his mother had ended up face-first in the cake. How old had he been? Six? After that, he'd said no thanks to efforts at celebration.

There. He'd "checked up" on her. Even that little bit of checking had triggered a bad memory, so he wanted to let it go there. Grace Day was doing well.

Still, even as he tried to tell himself he'd obeyed the letter of Graham's last instruction to him, it ate at the honor he had left. Rory had needed to see for himself that Gracie was doing all right. His last call had been a week ago.

And there had been *something* in her voice.

Even though she had said she was doing fabulously.

He couldn't pinpoint what exactly he had heard in her voice. A certain forced note to the breezy tone? Something guarded, as if she had a secret that she was not planning on revealing to him?

Whatever it was, it wouldn't let him go. Over the past week, the need to see her had grown in urgency. Instinct had become such a big part of his life when he was a soldier, that he found he couldn't ignore that niggling little voice. When he tried, it was just one more thing that woke him in the night, that haunted his dreams.

A little lie to her secretary had sent him to Pondview. "My company is one of the sponsors of Warrior Down. I need to talk to her urgently. And in person."

Just as he'd suspected, the mention of Gracie's pet project got him all the information he needed. Did he feel guilty for lying?

No. Guilt was for guys of a sensitive nature, and he definitely did not qualify. In his house, growing up, later on the battlefield, that was how you stayed alive. You didn't let things touch you.

But Graham dying... Rory shook it off, chose to focus with unnecessary intensity on Gracie. She was sneaking up on a fat black-and-white pony, who, while seeming oblivious, was clearly watching her out of the corner of his eye. She was right on one count: the pony *was* beady-eyed.

And a whole lot smarter than he looked. Because when she made her move, the pony sidled sideways, out of her grasp. He turned and looked at her balefully, chewing a clump of grass.

Rory winced when her heel embedded itself in the grassy ground, spongy from a recent watering and Gracie pitched forward. The heel snapped off her shoe with a click so audible Rory could hear it from where he was standing.

What was left of her cool reserve—and that wasn't much—abandoned her. Rory found himself smiling when she pried her foot free, took off a shoe and hurled it at the pony, who kicked up its heels at her and farted as it dodged the shoe.

"Bad horses become glue," she shouted. "And dog food. How would you like to be breakfast for a Great Dane?"

"Tut-tut," Rory muttered to himself. "Your decorum doesn't match your dress, Miss Day."

The truth? He liked the Miss Day who would throw a shoe at a pony much more than the one who answered her phone with such cool reserve, or the one who ran perfect birthday parties in her designer duds.

But then, he knew enough about the *real* Miss Day that she would be appalled. That's how bored guys whiled away their time. Played poker. Smoked. Slept. Talked.

About girlfriends and family.

Graham had never been that successful in the girl-friend department, so Rory knew an awful lot about his sister.

Like: *Gracie just never lets loose. You know, ever since she was a little girl she's carried a picture of a candy-apple red Ferrari. How did she become such a stick-in-the-mud? And how is it she's going to marry a stick-in-the-mud accountant, least likely ever to own a sports car? He drives a car that would barely make the economy class at a car-rental agency!*

Then, as if to prove her brother had her all wrong, that there was nothing stick-in-the-mud about her, Graham Day's straitlaced sister, who didn't know how to let loose, took off the other shoe and hurled it after the departing pony. She said a word—loudly—that soldiers used with fast and furious frequency but that would have raised a few eyebrows at her perfectly executed rich kids' birthday party.

Rory felt a smile tickle at his lips. A long, long time since he had found much to smile about.

Still, it was more than evident it was a bad time to talk to her. Of course, the chivalrous thing to do would be to rescue her, to save the day, but he had given up any illusions of being a hero long, long ago. And more, Gracie would *hate* his catching her like this.

In a bad spot.

Vulnerable.

Out of control.

Needing his help.

Besides, he didn't know anything about horses of the large variety, and less about the tiny ones.

Still, just leaving her to deal with it seemed too hard-hearted, even for him, the man generally untroubled by guilt.

But there it was: the memory of Graham required Rory to be a better man. Even if she was not his sister, Graham wouldn't have approved of abandoning the damsel in her distress.

Rory remembered he had a step up on the other heroes out there. A secret weapon. He pulled his cell phone from his pocket and tried not to wince when Bridey answered, halfway through the first ring, with her chipper, "Mr. Adams, sir."

He had tried to tell her his preference was for a more casual form of address, but on that topic she would not hear him.

Her tone reproachful, she was fond of reminding him, "Mr. Adams, you are the CEO of a very success-ful company."

"Bridey, I need you to find me someone who can round up some escaped ponies."

If the request took her by surprise, she certainly didn't let on. She took all the details and assured him she was on it.

Rory made a decision to help Gracie Day save whatever pride she had left by sinking further back into the shadows of the park, to be an interested spectator, nothing more.

But just as he made that decision, Gracie froze. It reminded him of a deer sniffing the air, some sense alerting it that it no longer was alone, that it was being observed. Then Gracie turned her head slowly and looked directly at him.

He saw recognition dawn in her eyes, and then in the set of her mouth.

She folded her arms over the green smudge on her chest and lifted her chin, trying for composure, distancing herself from that woman who had been hurling shoes and shouting invective at horses.

Taking a deep breath, feeling a sensation in his chest that was similar to what he felt just before starting the mission, just before stepping into the heat of battle, Rory Adams moved toward Gracie.

And stopped right in front of her.

Had he ever known her eyes were that color? He thought it was called hazel, a plain word for such a rich mix of golds and greens and browns worthy of an exotic tapestry.

Had he ever known that her lips were lush and wide? The kind of lips that a man imagined crushing under his own?

Of course he hadn't.

She had been a kid. His friend's sister.

Now she was a woman. A beautiful woman, if not a very happy one!

He hesitated, picked up her shoe—who said he couldn't be chivalrous?—and handed it to her.

"Hello, Gracie."

Grace Day blinked at the way her nickname sounded coming off his lips. *So right.*

As if part of her had ached to be called that again.

And, of course, part of her did. But by her brother. Not by Rory Adams.

She grabbed her shoe from his hand, and accidentally brushed his fingertips. The shock was electrical, and to hide its shiver from him, she shoved the shoe on her foot, buying a moment to breathe.

It had been eight years. Couldn't he be bald? Or fat? Couldn't life give her one little break?

She straightened, trying for dignity even though she was distinctly lopsided, and the narrow strap of her sundress chose that moment to slide down her shoulder.

Grace could clearly see that Rory Adams was *better* than he had been before. Twenty-one-year-old lankiness was gone, replaced with a male physique in its absolute prime. He was tall—well, he'd always been that, standing head and shoulders above his peers—but now he was also broad-shouldered and deep-chested.

He was wearing a sports shirt—short-sleeved— that showed off rock-hard biceps, the ripple of toned forearms. Khaki shorts hugged lean hips and powerful thighs, showed the naked length of his long, tanned legs.

His face had matured, too. She was not sure she would say it was better. *Changed.* The mischievousness of a young man was gone. So was the devil-may-care light that had always burned like fire in the depths of those green, green eyes.

Around his eyes, now, were the creases of a man who had squinted into the sun a great deal. There was a set to his jaw, a firmness around his mouth that had not been there before.

There was something in his expression that was closed and hard. It was the look of a warrior, a man who had accepted the mantle of serving his country, but at a price to himself. There were new shadows in eyes that had once been clear.

Rory Adams had seen things—and done things—that made the tatters of the birthday party behind her seem frivolous and superficial.

Her eyes wandered to his hair. It was brown, glossy and rich as a vat of melted dark chocolate, shining with the highlights of the Okanagan early summer sun.

The last time she had seen him, that dark hair had been very short, buzzed off to a mere shadow, vanity- and maintenance-free in preparation for hard, hot work in inhospitable climates.

Now, Rory had returned to a style closer to that she remembered from when he was coming in and out of their house with Graham.

Rory's family had moved onto their block and into their school district in the latter half of Graham's senior year. And then in those carefree days after they had finished high school, they had both worked for the same landscaping company.

That was before they had decided it was imperative that they go save the world.

Rory's hair was longer than it had been even then, longer than she had ever seen it, thick, rich, straight until it touched his collar, and then it curled slightly.

She supposed that's what everyone who got out of the military did—exercised the release from discipline, celebrated the freedom to grow their hair.

And yet the long hair did not make him look less a warrior, just a warrior from a different age.

Too easy to picture him with the long hair catching in the wind, that fierce expression on his face, a sword in his hand, *ready.*

He was the kind of man who made a woman feel the worst kind of weakness: a desire to feel his strength against her own softness, to feel the rasp of rough whiskers against delicate skin, to feel the hard line of those lips soften against her mouth.

But Rory Adams had always been that. Even now Grace could feel the ghost of the girl she had once been. She could feel the helpless humiliation she had felt at fourteen because she loved him so desperately.

And pathetically.

She'd been as invisible to him as a ghost. No, more like a mosquito, an annoyance he swatted at every now and then. His best friend's aggravating kid sister.

She'd known from the moment he had first called her six months ago, that nothing good could come from seeing him.

There had been something in his voice, grim and determined, that had made her think he had things to tell her that she was not ready to hear, that she would probably never be ready to hear.

Besides, seeing Rory? It could only make her yearn for things that could never be. She had never seen Rory without her brother, Graham.

The brother who was not coming home. Hadn't she thought seeing her brother's friend would intensify the sense of loss that was finally dulling to a throbbing ache instead of a screaming pain?

Once she had blamed this man who stood before her for Graham's choices, but a long time ago she had realized her brother had been born to do what he was doing. It was a choice that he had been willing to give his life for.

And he had.

But if Rory wanted to think she still held him responsible, and if it kept up some kind of barrier between them, that was okay.

Because what shocked Gracie right now was that what she felt looking at Rory was not an intensified sense of loss. Rather, she was unprepared for how the yearning of her younger self—to be noticed by him, to be cared about him—had not disappeared with her braces and her first bra.

Not even close.

She blinked. And then again, hard. "No one calls me that," she said. "No one calls me Gracie."

She thought she sounded childish and defensive. She didn't want him to know he'd had any kind of effect on her.

Why couldn't she just have said, "Hello, Rory. Nice to see you"? Why couldn't she have just said that, all her years of hard-won polish and sophistication wrapped around her like a protective cloak?

Because he had caught her in a terrible moment. Running after renegade ponies, her shoe broken, her hair clasp lost, her strap sliding around and her dress stained beyond repair.

If she'd known he wasn't going to take no for an answer, she would have invited him to the office she was so proud of on the main street of downtown Mason.

Where she could have been in complete control of this reunion!

"What do they call you?"

His voice was deep and sure and sent unwanted shivers down her spine.

Miss Day would have sounded way too churlish, plus she was wobbling on one shoe, and feeling damp and disheveled and not at all like the cool professional woman she wanted him to believe she was.

"Grace."

"Ah."

She didn't like the way he was looking at her, his gaze probing, those deep green eyes feeling as though they were stripping away her maturity and success and exposing the vulnerable and gauche girl she was so startled to find was alive and well within her.

"Graham's the only one who called me that. Everyone else called me Grace. Even my parents."

"Graham and me," he reminded her.

Gracie-Facie, pudding and pie, kissed the boys and made them cry...

On those rare occasions when Rory Adams had noticed her, it had been to tease her mercilessly.

But that boy who had teased—the one with the careless grin, and the wild way—seemed to be gone. Completely.

Why couldn't her inner child be so cooperative?

"So, how's life?" he said.

As if he'd just been walking by, and happened upon her. Which she doubted. When she'd talked to him a week ago, she'd told him she didn't want to see him.

She should have guessed that would not have changed about him. He was not a man who had had to accept no for an answer very often. Especially not from those of the female persuasion. She should have guessed he would not accept it from her.

"The same as when I talked to you a week ago," Grace said stubbornly. "Fabulous."

This was not true. In fact, nothing could be further from the truth.

"Except for the ponies," he commented dryly, but he she had a feeling he wasn't buying it, and not just because of the ponies. Not for a second.

Couldn't he see that her dress was perfectly cut fine linen? That the shoe he had handed her was an expensive designer shoe? Couldn't he see that she was all grown up and that she didn't need any help from big, strong him to get her through life's hurdles?

Of which, at the moment, she had more than her fair share.

"Fabulous," she repeated, tightly.

"You look worried," he said after a moment.

And then he did the darndest thing. He took his thumb, and ever so gently pressed it into her forehead.

Where she knew the worry lines had been building like storm clouds for a whole week!

Ever since Serenity had arrived with her entourage. Ponies. Tucker.

There was a momentary sensation of bliss: a momentary desire to lean into that thumb and all it offered. Someone to lean on. Someone to talk to. Someone to trust.

Hopeless illusions that she, of all people, should have left far behind her. The end of her engagement really should have been the last straw.

Had been the last straw, Grace told herself firmly. Her business was everything now. Everything. She had laid herself out on the altar of romantic love—and had been run through by love's caprice—for the last time.

She was not leaving herself open to hurt anymore. She had made that vow when her fiancé of two years, Harold, had bade her adieu. Vowed it.

And then, as if to test that vow, Serenity had come.

And now Rory was here. This man appearing in her life, her entertaining the notion it would be nice to hear his opinion about Serenity—or feel his whiskers scrape her face—those were tests of her resolve.

When he had phoned, she had contemplated asking him a few questions, but in the end she had decided not to.

And the deep cynicism that permeated his expression should only confirm how right she had been in that decision.

Because he could lay her hope to rest. Dash it completely before it was even fully formed.

Hope was such a fragile thing for her.

Hope was probably even more dangerous to her than love. But still, not to hope for anything at all would be a form of death, wouldn't it?

She was not about to trust her hope to someone like him. And yet, there it was—the temptation just to tell him, to see what he thought.

Not to be so damned alone.

Recognizing the utter folly of these thoughts, Grace slapped his thumb down from her forehead. "I'm not worried."

No sense giving in to the temptation to share confidences, to tell him she'd spent years building up her business. One incident like this, and it could all crumble, word spreading like wildfire that she was unprofessional, that she'd had a disaster.

Thank goodness the party had been over, the last of the pint-size revelers being packed into their upscale minivans and SUVs when the ponies had made their break for it. Hopefully the park people—or the press— wouldn't come along before she got this cleared up.

But that was only the immediate problem, anyway, although all her problems were related at the moment.

"Didn't the ponies come with a pony person?" he asked.

Ah, that was the other problem. The pony person was exactly the secret she wanted to keep.

"The pony person is, um, incapacitated. Not your problem," she said, flashing him a smile that made him frown. She had been aiming for a smile that said, *This? Just a temporary glitch. Nothing I can't handle.*

And she had obviously missed *that* smile by a long

shot. Grace hoped he didn't catch her anxious glance toward the parking lot.

Thankfully, she'd had the trailer the ponies had arrived in moved way across the parking lot into the deep shade of the cottonwoods on the other side. She had not wanted the partygoers to bump right into it in its decrepit condition.

"Maybe we'll meet again under different circumstances," she said, hoping he would take the hint and leave.

But he did not have the look of a man who responded to subtlety, and he had caught her glance toward the parking lot. Now he was looking past her. She moved in front of him, trying to block his view, but it was no use. He looked over her head, easily.

Not a single person at the party had mentioned the trailer. It was as if they hadn't seen it at all.

But then, most people weren't like him.

And Rory Adams had become a man who saw everything, who missed absolutely nothing.

Of course, she knew from the few things Graham had said when he came home on leave that these men led lives that depended on their ability to be observant of their surroundings, every nuance of detail, every vehicle, every person, every obstacle.

Rory stepped around her, and headed right toward where the ramshackle horse trailer was. It was painted a shade of copper that almost hid the rust eating away at it around the wheel wells.

On the side, in fading circus letters, three feet high, it said, Serenity's Wild Ride.

He looked over his shoulder at Grace, his eyes narrow. "What's she doing here?"

He recognized the trailer. He knew Serenity. Was it what Grace feared? Or what she hoped?

CHAPTER TWO

"You know her," Grace said, scrambling to keep up with him on her one shoe. "You know Serenity."

She stopped and picked up the other on her way. Since one had a heel and the other didn't, she took them both off and dangled them from her fingertips.

"A chance encounter a long, long time ago." Rory glanced back at her, hesitated, and then waited. "Watch for pony poo."

"Oh!" Life was so unfair. Well, that was hardly a newsflash. But, if Grace had to see Rory Adams, wouldn't it have been nice if she had been sipping a glass of white wine and looking entirely unflappable, rather than chasing after him in bare feet, avoiding poo?

"What's she doing here, Gracie?"

She wanted to remind him she didn't want to be called Gracie, but something about the way Rory had stopped and was looking down at her made her feel very flustered.

The weak compulsion to share the burden won.

"She came by the office a week ago."

"She knew where your office was," he said flatly.

"I'm in the phone book. She said she knew Graham."

Grace did not miss how his eyes narrowed at that.

"She knew I had an event company."

"So, she's done some homework."

"You don't need to make it sound like she's running a sting, and she found an easy mark."

He raised an eyebrow. It said *exactly*.

"She just wondered if I could give her some work. She had ponies, I had an upcoming birthday party. It seemed like it might be win-win."

"What aren't you telling me?"

Hell's bells. She did not like it that he could see through her that easily. It meant she had to avoid looking at his lips.

Naturally, as soon as she told herself not to look at his lips, she did just that. Why did men like him have this kind of seductive power over people? Female people anyway!

"What makes you think I'm not telling you something?" she hedged.

"I was Graham's best friend for ten years and you refused to see me, but a complete stranger shows up who claims a passing acquaintance to your brother and you're forming a business partnership with her?"

"I rented her ponies for an afternoon. That's hardly a business partnership."

"It's not 'I can't see why we need to talk,' either."

Something crossed his face.

"I hurt your feelings," Grace said, stunned.

For a moment, he looked stunned, too. Then a shield came down over his eyes, making them seem a darker shade of emerald than they had before. A little smile tickled the sinfully sensuous curve of his mouth. His expression was not exactly amusement, and not exactly scorn. More a kind of deprecating self-knowledge.

"Gracie, honey—"

Gracie wasn't bad enough? Now he had to add honey to it?

"I don't have feelings for you to hurt."

That was what he wanted for her to believe. And she saw it was entirely possible that he believed that himself. But she didn't.

And suddenly Rory Adams was more dangerous to her than ever. Because he wasn't just handsome. He wasn't just the first man she'd ever had a crush on. He wasn't just her brother's best friend and fellow adventurer.

Because just before that shield had come down in his eyes, Grace was sure she had caught a glimpse of someone who had lost their way, someone who relied totally on himself, someone lonely beyond what she had ever known that word to mean.

"There was a complication," she admitted slowly. "That's why I agreed to have her provide ponies for the party."

"The thing about a woman like Serenity?"

She hated the way he said that, as if he knew way too much about women in general and women like Serenity in particular.

"What kind of woman is Serenity?" Grace demanded sweetly, though the kind of woman Serenity was was terribly obvious, even to Grace. Serenity was one of those women who had lived hard and lived wild, and it was all catching up with her.

The line around Rory's lip tightened as he decided

what to say. "She's the kind who used to own the party," he said. "And then the party owned her."

Grace suspected that he had sugarcoated what he really wanted to say, but what he had said was harsh enough, and it was said with such a lack of sympathy that the moment of unwanted—and weakening sympathy she had felt for him—evaporated.

Thank God.

"And what about women like Serenity?" she said, yanking her strap up one more time.

"There's always a complication."

Then he strode over to the horse trailer, and Gracie could not help but notice he was all soldier now, totally focused, totally take-charge and totally no-nonsense.

It felt like a terrible weakness on her part that she was somewhat relieved both by the fact his armor was back up and by the fact he was taking charge.

So she had to say, "I can handle this."

He snorted, glanced meaningfully at the pony in the wading pool, trampling what was left of the soggy Happy Birthday banner, and said, "Sure you can, Gracie."

I hurt your feelings. Really, Gracie Day couldn't have picked a more annoying thing to say to him.

Feelings? Weren't those the pesky things that he'd managed to outrun his whole life? Starting with a less than stellar childhood—no ponies at birthday parties, for sure—and ending up in a profession where to feel anything too long or too intensely would have meant he couldn't do his job.

No, Rory Adams was a man ideally suited for soldiering. His early life had prepared him for hardship. The little bit of idealism that he had managed to escape his childhood with had soon departed, too.

So, Rory Adams had *hated* the look in Gracie's eyes, just now, doe-soft, as if she could see right through him.

To some secret longing.

To have what she and Graham had had. Their house the one on the block that everyone flocked to, and not just because there were always freshly baked choco-late chip cookies, either. There was something there. That house was full of laughter. And love. Parents who actually made rules and had dinner on the table at a certain time.

Rory remembered calling Graham once about a party. And Graham saying, "Nah, I'm going fishing with my dad."

A family that enjoyed being together. That had been a novelty in Rory Adam's world.

Is that what he'd wanted when he'd called her? Had it been about him and not about her—or his obligation to Graham—at all?

No, he reminded himself. He'd been *relieved* by her rejection.

Rory shrugged off the thoughts, annoyed with him-self. He was not accustomed to questioning himself or his motives. Except for the event that haunted his dreams, he moved through life with the supreme con-fidence of the warrior he was. The qualities that had made him an exceptional warrior also made him good at business.

So it flustered him beyond reason that a single glance from her had shaken something deep, deep within him.

He drew in a long breath, steadying himself, clearing away distractions, focusing on what needed to be done.

Poking out from underneath the horse trailer, near the back bumper, was one very tiny, suede, purple cowboy boot, with a fake spur attached.

He nudged at the boot with his shoe and then a little harder when there was no response. The boot moved away.

Sighing, he bent down and tugged. And this time he met some real resistance.

He felt under the trailer, found the other boot and pulled. Out came long, naked legs, and then short denim shorts, frayed at the cuffs, and then a bare belly, and then a sequined pop top with fringes. And then the face of an angel—if it weren't for the circles of black mascara under her eyes—and blond curls topped with a pink cowboy hat.

He studied her for a moment. Despite her prettiness, she was aging badly. He and Graham had partied—hard—with her and her rodeo crowd. They'd been a rowdy, rough bunch. It had been a brief interlude—a few crazy days before their unit had mustered out the very first time.

That made it eight years ago, about the same amount of time since he had seen Gracie in her braces.

But whereas Grace had come into herself, Serenity had deteriorated badly. She must have been in her twenties at that first encounter, which meant she was way too old now to be wearing short shorts and a pink cowboy hat. She was on the scary side of skinny, her hair had been bleached once too often, and she was definitely drunk.

Well, that part was the same.

"Leave me alone," the black-eyed angel mumbled, swinging at air.

"Yes, leave her alone," Gracie said. "Really, there's nothing here I can't handle."

He ignored them both.

"Look, Rory, you just don't understand the delicate nuances of this situation."

"Uh-huh," he said, but he was pretty sure he got the "delicate nuances" just fine. Serenity had probably come across the obituary for Graham somewhere, and zeroed in on the grieving sister.

It made him mad, but one thing that the military had been really good at was training him to channel aggression, control it, unleash it only as a last resort.

So he satisfied himself with giving Gracie a sour look that let her know he was not impressed with how she had handled this so far.

And he was rewarded with a look that had nothing doe-soft about it.

"There's nothing here I can't handle," she said, again.

"Given that this woman is bad, bad news and her ponies are devouring Mason's most prime real estate, you might want to consider the possibility you are in over your head."

Her mouth worked, but she didn't say anything. He could tell that Gracie had suspected Serenity was exactly what he said. Bad news.

And she had suspected that she was in over her head.

But there was something else, too, something glittering at the back of her eyes that gave him pause.

For some reason she *wanted* Serenity here.

What did Serenity have to offer that Grace had rejected from him?

Sheesh. His damn feelings *were* hurt. That was a stunner. A weakness about himself that he could have lived quite happily not knowing he had!

"Hey," he reached down and took Serenity's shoulder. "Wake up, get your ponies and clear out."

The attack came from the side. At first, confused, Rory thought it was Grace who had hurled herself at him, nearly pushed him over.

He stumbled a step sideways, straightened and felt a warrior's embarrassment at not even having seen the attacker coming, at having been caught off guard.

It made it worse, not better, that his attacker was pint-size.

The attacker aimed a hard kick with cowboy-boot-clad feet at Rory's shin. Still slightly off guard, Rory shot out his arm and held the child at arm's length. The kick missed but, undeterred, the kid tried again.

A boy. Rory had not been around children much, so he didn't know how old. Seven? Eight? Maybe nine?

Despite his size, the boy had the slouch and confidence of a professional wrangler. And he was dressed like one, too. His jeans had holes in both knees, his denim shirt had been washed white. A stained cowboy hat was pulled low over his brow. It was more than obvious this child had not been at the upscale birthday party that had just ended.

"Don't you ever touch my mama," he said, glaring up at Rory, not the least intimidated by the fact his opponent was taller than him by a good three feet and outweighed him by about a hundred and fifty pounds.

He was the kind of kid—spunky, undernourished, defiant—that you could care about.

If you hadn't successfully killed the part of yourself that cared about such things. Rory had seen lots of kids like this: chocolate-brown eyes, white, white smiles, spunk, and he'd learned quickly you couldn't allow yourself to care. The world was too full of tragedy. It could overwhelm you if you let it.

Rory let go of the boy, backed away, hands held up in surrender. "Hey, I was just trying to rouse her so she could catch her ponies."

"I'll look after the ponies," the boy said fiercely.

"It's okay, Tucker," Gracie said, and put a hand on the boy's narrow shoulders. "Nobody's going to hurt your mother."

The boy flinched out from her touch and glared out at her from under the battered rim of his straw cowboy hat with such naked dislike that Rory saw Gracie suck in her breath.

Rory looked at the boy more closely.

And then Rory looked at Gracie's face.

She was clearly struggling to hide everything from him, and she was just as clearly a person who had never learned to keep her distance from caring. Her tenderness toward that boy was bald in her face. And so was the hope.

But she hid nothing at all.

Rory Adams was a man who had lived by his instincts, by his ability to distance himself from emotion. He had survived because of his ability to be observant, to see what others might overlook.

Rory looked back and forth between the boy and Grace, and he saw immediately what the complication was.

He studied the boy—Tucker—hard.

"How old are you?"

Grace gasped, seeing how quickly he had seen the possibility.

The boy did not look like Graham. But he certainly looked like Grace had looked just a few years older than this: freckle-faced and auburn hair.

A million kids looked like that.

For a moment, Rory thought the boy wasn't going to answer him at all.

From Serenity, a moan, and then, "Come on, Tuck, tell the man how old you are."

"I'm seven," he said, reluctance and belligerence mixed in equal parts.

So, there it was. A little quick math and the complication became a little more complicated, a little more loaded with possibility. And Grace was clinging to that possibility like a sailor to a raft in shark-infested waters.

Serenity crawled back under the truck.

"I need to talk to you," he said, grimly, to Grace. He pointed at the boy. "And you need to go catch those ponies."

"You're not the boss over me," Tucker said.

The flash in his eyes and the tilt of his chin were identical to those of the woman beside him.

And the defiance was likable, if you were open to that kind of thing. Which, Rory reminded himself, he wasn't.

"You're the one who said you'd look after the po-

nies," Rory reminded him. Tucker left, making it clear
with one black backward glance it was his choice to go.

When he was gone, Rory turned his full attention
to Gracie, whose expression clearly said he was not the
boss over her, either.

"Did Serenity tell you that kid was Graham's?"

"Don't call him that kid! His name is Tucker."

"Okay," he said, feeling how forced his patience was,
"did she tell you Tucker was Graham's?"

"No." That very recognizable tilt of chin.

"Did she insinuate it?"

"No. I had them over for dinner the other night. She
never said a word about Graham and Tucker. Not one
word."

"You had them over for dinner? At your house?"

The you're-not-the-boss-over-me expression deepened. Rory had to fight an urge to shake her. All those
years of discipline being tried by a hundred-and-ten-
pound woman!

"Why wouldn't I have them over for dinner?"

*Because it's akin to throwing a bucket of fish guts to
seagulls. They'll be back.* He said nothing.

"I actually enjoyed it. She's had a very tough life,
but she's very interesting."

"You don't know anything about her!"

Her chin was tilting stubbornly.

"You can't save the whole world, Gracie."

"No? Isn't that what you and Graham were so fired
up to do?"

He let that bounce off him, like a fighter who had
only been nudged by a blow that could have killed had
it landed.

His voice cold, he said, "That's precisely why I know it can't be done."

Instead of having the good sense to see what he was trying to tell her—that he was hard and cold and mean—that soft look was in her eyes again.

It made him wonder if maybe, just maybe, if she couldn't save the whole world, if she could save one person.

And if that person was him.

The thought stunned him. It had never occurred to him he needed to be saved. From what?

"You want desperately for that boy to be Graham's," he said softly.

"Don't you? Don't you want some part of Graham to go on?"

He heard the desperation, the pure emotion, and knew he could not rely on her to make any rational decisions.

"Look, the things that made Graham who he was are not exactly purely genetic. Those things are the result of how the two of you were raised."

He remembered her family. Off to church on Sunday mornings. Going to their cabin on the lake together. Playing board games on winter nights. Lots of hugs and hair-ruffling. Their parents had given them so much love and affection.

He was trying to tell her that the way that Tucker was being raised he didn't have a hope of turning out anything like Graham. Even if he was Graham's, which was a pretty big if.

"It's easy enough to find out," he said. "Whether he's Graham's or not."

She said nothing.

"A cotton swab, the inside of his cheek, an envelope, a result."

"Good grief, how often have you done that?" she said with scorn, but he knew it was to hide the fact it frightened her that it was that easy.

He didn't say anything. Let her believe what she wanted. Especially if it killed the soft look in her eyes, which it did.

"Don't you want to know the truth about Tucker?" he asked.

"Yes! But I want Serenity to tell me the truth!"

"You want Serenity to tell you the truth?" he asked, incredulous. Was it possible to be this hopelessly naive?

Grace nodded, stubborn.

"You know how you can tell Serenity is lying?"

"How?"

"Her lips are moving."

"That's unnecessarily cynical."

"There is no such thing as being unnecessarily cynical."

She glared at him then changed tack. "How well did you and Graham know her?"

"Well enough to know she'll tell you whatever you want to hear if there's money involved."

"You're hopelessly distrustful."

"Yeah. And alive. And those two things are not mutually exclusive. Grace, there's a woman lying under a trailer, presumably drunk. Her ponies are all over the park. If ever there was a call to cynicism, this is it."

Suddenly, the defiance left her expression. He wished

he'd had time to get ready for what she did next. Grace laid her hand on his wrist.

Everything she was was in that touch. The way she was dressed tried to say one thing about her: that she was a polished and successful businesswoman.

At least before her pony encounter.

But her touch said something entirely different. She probably would have been shocked by how her touch told her truth.

That she was gentle, a little naive, hopeful about life. She was too soft and too gullible. He was not sure how she had managed that. To remain that through life's tragedies, the death of her brother, the breakup of her engagement.

There was a kind of courage in it that he reluctantly admired even while he felt honor-bound to discourage it.

She looked at him, and there was pleading in her eyes. "I know you're just trying to protect me. But please, Rory, let me do this my way. Is it so terrible to want a miracle?"

Miracles. He'd never been a man with any kind of faith, and spending all his adult life in war zones had not improved his outlook in that department. He—from a family who had never set foot in a church—had said his share of desperate prayers.

His last one had been *Don't let this man, my friend, die.*

He both admired her hope, and wanted to kill it before it got away on her and did some serious damage.

Trying for a gentle note, which was as foreign to him as speaking Chinese, Rory said, "Gracie, come on. No one walks on water."

At that moment, a pickup truck shot into the parking lot, and pulled up beside the horse trailer. It had a decal on the side for the Mountain Retreat Guest Ranch. A cowboy got out of the driver's side.

He looked as though he was straight off a movie set. Booted feet, plaid shirt, Stetson, fresh-faced and clean-scrubbed. Three other cowboys spilled out the open doors.

"Slim McKenzie," the first one said. "I hear you're having a pony problem."

Gracie turned and looked at Rory, those amazing eyes dancing with the most beautiful light.

"Maybe no one walks on water," she said, quietly, "But garden-variety miracles happen all the time."

He wanted to ask her where the damned miracle had been for her brother. But he found, to his dismay, he was not quite hard-hearted enough to be the one to snuff out that light in her eyes.

And the light in her eyes was doing the strangest thing to him. He knew the arrival of the cowboys was no miracle, not of the garden variety or any other. It was the Bridey variety miracle, pure and simple.

But something was happening nonetheless. Unless he was mistaken, Gracie's light was piercing the darkness in him, bringing brightness to a place that had not seen it for a long, long time.

He did not allow himself to marvel at it. He thrust the feeling of warmth away. His darkness could put out her light in a millisecond.

And he'd better remember that when he was thinking about how beautiful Graham's kid sister had become.

CHAPTER THREE

GRACE watched with absolute delight as the angels who had arrived dressed as cowboys rounded up the ponies. How could Rory not believe in miracles?

In less than an hour the whole disaster was not just repaired, it was practically erased.

It also took less than an hour to become very evident to her that Rory Adams might not know a thing about ponies, but leadership came as naturally to him as breathing.

"How about if you just sit this one out?" Rory had suggested with a meaningful look at her damaged footwear.

She could have resented how he took over from her, but frankly she was sick to death of ponies, and though it was probably a crime in the career woman's manual, she reluctantly admitted it was somewhat of a relief to have someone take over. But not out loud.

Rory set up an impromptu command center, and she found, in her softened frame of mind, with him unaware of her scrutiny, it was nice to watch him.

Rory Adams was a force unto himself, pure masculine energy practically sizzled in the air around him. He came up with a plan, quickly, delegated, and then he pitched in. He was afraid of nothing: not ponies racing straight at him, not being dragged on the other end of a rope by a tiny pony that was much stronger than seemed possible.

From a purely feminine point of view, watching Rory was enough to make her mouth go dry. He was agile, energetic and strong. It seemed every muscle he possessed was being tested to its rather magnificent limits. Every now and then his shout of command—or laughter—would ring out across the field.

When a pony charged in her direction, he threw himself at it, glancing off its shoulder, but managing to change its direction.

And then he rolled easily to his feet—as if he had not just risked life and limb to save her—and kept moving.

It occurred to her that he protected in the same way he led. It came to him as naturally as breathing.

And it felt like the most terrible of weaknesses that it made her insides turn to jelly.

Within an hour the last of the ponies was loaded into the ramshackle trailer. The poop was scooped. The birthday banner was fished out of the pool. Serenity was installed in the backseat of her crew-cab truck, and Tucker, looking at home for the first time since she had met him, was sandwiched in between two large cowboys on the front seat.

"Clayton and Sam will drive their truck to wherever they want to go," Slim said, addressing Rory. "I'll follow in my truck."

There was something in the way he was addressing Rory, with a respectful kind of deference, that gave her pause. A suspicion whispered to life inside her, and

Grace could feel the pink cloud she had been floating on since the timely arrival of the cowboys evaporating beneath her.

"Anything else you need done, Mr. Adams?"

Mr. Adams? Grace tried to think whether there had been an exchange of names in the flurry of activity that had begun since those cowboys first rolled up. Certainly, she had not given her name.

She felt as if she was on red alert now, watching Rory even more intently than she had been when he was commanding the field. Maybe she didn't know him that well, and maybe many years had gone by since she had seen him, but he simply was not the kind of man who would introduce himself as Mr. Adams.

It was the kind of thing Harold might have done: trying to one-up himself over simple, working men, but Rory would *never* do that.

She told herself it was impossible to know that given the shortness and circumstances of their reacquaintance, but it didn't matter. Her heart said it knew.

Still, instead of feeling a soft spot for him, she reminded herself something was up, there was more going on here than met the eye.

Rory, catching her sudden intense focus on him, clapped the cowboy on the shoulder and moved off into the distance, where she couldn't hear what they said.

But she was pretty sure that was a wallet coming out of Rory's back pocket!

By the time he came back, any admiration she had felt about his camaraderie with the working man was gone. So was her pink cloud.

In fact, Grace felt as if she had landed back on earth

with a rather painful thump. She should have never let her barriers down by admiring him, not even discreetly! Now she had to build them back up. Why was that always harder than taking them down?

The trucks pulled out of the park, the horse trailer swaying along behind them, with great clinking and clanking and whinnying of ponies.

And then there was silence. And Rory standing beside her, surveying the park and looking way too pleased with himself.

"That wasn't a miracle, was it?" she demanded.

"I don't know. Eight ponies successfully captured in—" he glanced at his watch "—under eight minutes per pony. Might qualify. Did I mention I'm no expert on miracles?"

He was looking at her, his expression boyishly charming, though there was something in his eyes that was guarded.

"I meant the arrival of Slim and the gang."

He was very silent. And now he looked away from her, off into the distance. He wouldn't look at her.

"It wasn't even the garden-variety kind, was it?"

Silence.

"Why didn't you say something instead of letting me prattle on?" *Instead of letting me believe.*

"Aw, Gracie," he said, finally looking back at her, "you're too old to believe in stuff like that, anyway."

She blinked. "I'm *old?*"

"Not old as in decrepit." His look was intense, and then he said softly, "Not at all."

Grace recognized how easy it would to be charmed by him. And she recognized he was a man who had been charming his way past the ruffled feathers of the female species since he'd been old enough to blink that dark tangle of lashes over those sinfully green eyes.

And that after he'd been the one to ruffle the feathers!

"I just meant the last time I saw you, you were a little girl. You probably still believed in Santa Claus."

"I was fourteen! I certainly did not believe in Santa Claus." Though she had been hopelessly in love with the man who stood before her, imagining endless scenarios where he finally *saw* her. And that was probably exactly the kind of magical thinking he thought she was too old for now.

And he was right.

Somehow the hurt of being invisible to him all those years ago, and this moment of his debunking her desire to believe in miracles were fusing together, and she could feel her temper rising.

"What did you have to do with those men arriving?" she demanded.

"I saw you were having trouble. I made a phone call."

"What kind of man can make a phone call and have a truckload of cowboys delivered?"

"You needn't say it as if it were a truckload of bootleg liquor during prohibition and you were leading the group of biddies waving a sign saying liquor is of the devil."

"Old and prim," she said dangerously.

"You do have a little pinched look around your mouth that reminds me of a schoolteacher who has found a frog in her drawers."

She sputtered with outrage.

"Hey. Desk drawers!"

"Stop it! You're trying to distract me."

"Is it working?" he said silkily.

Yes. "No!"

"Because I have another way to take that pinched look off your lips. Not to mention distract you."

Rory Adams was threatening her with a kiss!

And it was far too easy to imagine the hard line of those lips dropping over the softness of her own!

She stared at him, and then felt the traitorous blush moving up her neck. She didn't blush anymore. Who blushed in this day and age? Oh God, she was acting exactly like the old biddy he'd accused her of being.

Then she realized he had no intention of *really* kissing her. He was teasing her the same way he had when she was a child. And she had the frustrating feeling he was still enjoying the result!

She drew in a deep breath, did her best to erase kisses from her mind. "Quit dodging the issue. What I want to know is how you happened to be here at the park as all this was unfolding?"

"Just as you found yourself in need of a white knight?" he asked.

He was baiting her. Wanting her to argue about his qualifications to be a white knight. Or maybe about hers to be a damsel in distress.

But she wasn't fourteen anymore, and she was not going to allow him to suck her into his teasing. Or to look at his lips and wish, in a moment of madness, that he hadn't been teasing about his ability to distract with *that.*

She folded her arms over her smudged chest and

tapped her foot. She told herself she didn't care if she looked like an old-biddy schoolmarm with a frog in her drawers.

"What were you doing here?"

"Your secretary told me where I could find you," he admitted.

Grace felt a moment's annoyance at her secretary, Beth, but it quickly dissipated. What woman would have a chance against Rory if he decided to turn on his charm? Including her. So she steeled herself against him, kept her arms folded and her foot tapping.

"And why did you want to find me?"

"We have some business to discuss."

"I already told you we didn't."

"Well, now we do."

"You're right. Send me a bill and I'll reimburse you for whatever you paid to have the ponies rounded up."

He looked scornful. "That's never going to happen."

"Then we have no business. I'd like to say it was nice seeing you again, but the circumstances overshadow the delight, I'm afraid. Good-bye and—"

"My company wants to be one of the sponsors for your fundraising event for Warrior Down. We're prepared to make a substantial contribution."

Now he had truly caught her off guard. Her arms dropped and her foot stopped tapping.

A stronger woman would have refused him outright. But Warrior Down was her baby. Of all the events she would plan this year, only this one would be so close to her heart. Its success meant everything to her. Everything.

As much as she wanted to, she could not put her own

pride in front of her cause. How could she say no to a man who could pull cowboys out of thin air? She was pretty sure any contribution he wanted to make to Warrior Down was going to be amazing, because he was not a man who would ever be satisfied with the ordinary.

Including an ordinary girl like you, she thought, and then pushed that thought away like a pesky fly.

She wanted to know right now what he considered a substantial contribution, but she also had the horrible feeling of the balance of power shifting to him, and she'd had enough of him having the upper hand for one day.

She was not going to address this situation while standing here in the growing afternoon heat of the park in a broken shoe and a smudged dress. She was not in any kind of frame of mind to make good decisions, never mind maintain absolute control over her baby, Warrior Down.

She could barely defend herself against his teasing!

No, she needed time to repair herself. And prepare herself for whatever he had to propose.

She was going to meet him on her own ground.

After she'd had a chance to regain her composure. Not to mention have her hair done and her best outfit on. The next time she saw Rory Adams she would have her best foot forward! She would not be a woman flustered by the insinuation of a kiss!

She smiled with as much professionalism as she could muster. "I'd be delighted to discuss that with you. If you'll call my secretary, Beth, she'll make an appointment for you."

He looked shocked that she was putting him off. He

wasn't used to not having his way, and that was just too damned bad.

She turned and limped away with as much dignity as she could muster.

"Hey, Gracie-Facie."

She looked over her shoulder and glared at him.

"You could say thanks for the help."

For a delicious moment, she thought she had gotten to him. That he had expected her to fall all over herself in gratitude for being rescued by him, that he was actually flustered by a woman who did not succumb to his charms.

But she saw, in that glance back, that he was not the least perturbed by her lack of gratitude.

That he was amused by it. And by her. The same way as he had been when she was that little girl he had tormented by calling her Gracie-Facie instead of falling madly in love with her.

Gracie-Facie, indeed!

Well, next time they were meeting on her turf, and everything was going to be under her control. She would be completely cool, calm, collected, professional. Completely.

But for a woman who wanted to be completely cool, calm, collected and professional, she actually had to bite down on her lip to keep from sticking her tongue out at him.

And his shout of laughter, as if he could see right through her, shivered along her spine.

Rory did not look as if he laughed like that very much anymore.

Grace recognized it as a dangerous weakness, that

after all the fun he'd had at her expense, she was actually glad she had made him laugh, glad she could pull from him, even for a second, a shadow of the carefree young man he had once been.

Rory watched her go, the smile still tickling his lips.

Given that he considered himself a man generally unencumbered by touchy-feely sentiments like guilt, he was just a little amazed by how relieved he was to be turning the little white lie he'd told her secretary into a truth.

Offering to do something for Warrior Down was the carrot Grace Day could not resist.

The fact was, he already knew it was not going to be that smart to tangle their lives together. She was sensitive, sweet, feisty, smart—in other words, way more complicated than the kind of woman he was used to.

She also was way more innocent than anybody he was accustomed to dealing with. Her face had turned the color of a fire hydrant when he had said he knew just how to wipe that prissy look off her face!

His own reaction to the thought of kissing her had been anything but playful.

On the other hand, she was in way over her head with the whole Serenity thing, and he was not cutting her loose to deal with it herself. Warrior Down would be the perfect excuse to keep tabs on her.

And he hoped she would never find out what he had just asked that cowboy.

She probably would have no objection to the fact he had asked to be informed about where Serenity and Tucker and their eight ponies were living and how, but it was the other part that would probably put her nose seriously out of joint.

Buy the kid a can of soda pop on the way to wherever they're going. Keep the can.

Grace wanted to play it one way with Serenity and that was okay *for her.* But Rory needed to have a backup plan in case hers didn't pan out, which he was fairly certain it wasn't going to.

Serenity was going to play her hand close to her chest and milk it for all it was worth. If Tucker was Graham's, wouldn't Serenity have said so already? Why wouldn't she have told Graham while he was alive? What would be the benefit to her of keeping the boy a secret?

Rory watched Grace toodle out of the parking lot in one of those big luxury cars you associated with an old person who was sending the message *I've made it.* She looked cautiously right and left, careful not to even glance in his direction.

Make an appointment with my secretary.

Grace thought it was all going to go her way next time, that she was inviting him into her uptight little world where she would have all the control.

The thing was, from everything Graham had told him about her, the last thing Gracie needed was more control.

Hey, he warned himself, *getting way too involved here.*

But what if Graham hadn't meant just check on her? What if that was too literal? What if he had really meant, check on her and if there is a little tightness around her mouth and still shadows of sorrow in her eyes, and if she's trying to control everything in the whole world, do something about it?

Rory sighed. He was the man least qualified to interpret a dying man's last words.

But he was pretty sure Graham would approve of him shaking up Gracie's world just a bit. And even if Graham didn't, a little part of Rory was looking forward to it. And so it just wasn't going to go her way.

And though she was unlikely to recognize it at first, that was going to be his gift to her, the kid sister of his deceased best friend. Maybe he didn't actually have to burden her with the details of his part in Graham's death. Maybe he just had to try to make up for it.

And, unreasonably pleased with himself, Rory was pretty sure he knew just how to shake up Gracie's tidy little world.

He took his cell phone out of his pocket and dialed the office of Day of Our Lives. He made his appointment for the next day. And then he called Bridey. His personal assistant would be earning her money today.

"Mr. Adams, *sir.*"

Rory winced. "Great job on the cowboys, Bridey. How did you do that?"

"Thank you, sir. Mr. McKenzie is a nice young man. I spent a weekend at his guest ranch not long ago. I'm afraid it's not faring that well with the poor economy."

"I gave him another little job to do, so maybe that will help. And I've got another challenge for you. I need you to find something for me by tomorrow. It's not going to be easy."

Bridey sighed with rich contentment. "Not easy is my favorite," she told him.

He told her what he needed. He waited for her to gasp, for her to tell him that finally he had given her a task she could not complete, that it was impossible.

Instead, completely unfazed, Bridey said, "Italia or Spider?"

Grace had been slightly taken aback to return to her office and find Rory had already made an appointment to see her. Had she known he was going to be that prompt she could have forewarned Beth to put him off for at least a few days!

Still, by the next morning Grace felt as ready for Rory Adams as a woman could ever feel ready for a man like that.

She looked around her office with satisfaction. The space was not ostentatious, but it was tastefully decorated to welcome clients. Her desk was antique mahogany, the two chairs on the other side of it were deeply comfortable distressed leather. The art was local, the rugs were imported. Like her car, it all whispered, subtly, *arrived.*

Still, Beth had sniffed the air this morning and asked if she was planning on doing surgery in here.

"What does that mean?"

"I don't know. It looks sterile. It smells antiseptic."

Sterile and antiseptic weren't quite the impressions Grace was looking for, so she had ordered herself an arrangement of white lilies and placed them artfully on the corner of her desk.

When they'd asked her at the florists what to put on the card, at first she had said no card. But then it had occurred to her: what would it hurt for a card to be inserted amongst the fragrant blossoms? Just in case he happened to glance that way? He was a detail guy. The type who saw everything.

So, it would be good for him to see a lovely bouquet with a card addressed in masculine handwriting that said, *To Gracie, with love.*

When the bouquet had arrived she looked at the card and wondered if it foreshadowed things not going quite as per her plan, because there was nothing masculine about the handwriting. So she took out the card and tossed it.

Unnecessary attention to detail, maybe, but this was, after all, what she did for a living. Staged perfect events.

Though it was not completely lost on her that the fact she was going to all this trouble to manipulate his impressions of her already meant she was in trouble of some sort.

And it wasn't just the freshly cleaned office and the flowers, either.

No, a nearly sleepless night planning what to wear, in her tired mind trying on and discarding nearly every outfit she owned.

She had settled on the light wool Chanel suit in a shade of turquoise that reminded her of an ice-wine bottle. Secretly she called it her "sexy librarian" outfit. Which was exactly the look she wanted: looking sexy at the same time as looking as though she had made no effort to do so. Under the jacket she had on a navy blue silk blouse, very professional, even with the buttons undone one lower than normal.

"For the *very* sexy librarian look," she said.

The outfit was obviously way too warm for the hot

summer weather, but the office was air-conditioned, and observant as he was, Rory Adams wouldn't know wool from hemp.

So, unlike their last meeting, this time everything was perfect.

Her hair was pinned up, her makeup was subtle but flattering, the outfit was professional with the tiniest hint of sexy, and the atmosphere was one-hundred-percent successful businesswoman. Grace even had a script of sorts figured out.

So, what exactly did you have in mind for sponsorship? A cash donation would work best for us.

At precisely eleven o'clock, Beth came in the door, closed it behind her, leaned on it.

"Ohmygod, he's here."

There was no question who *he* was. Beth's faintly dazed expression said it all.

Annoyed at her secretary's easy capitulation to Rory's considerable charms, Grace was even more determined to remain as icy cool as the color of her dress.

"Who is here?" she asked coolly, hoping to prompt professionalism. Beth, naturally, ignored the coolness. They were a two-woman office, which over the years had made them so much more than employer and employee. They were friends and coworkers. Beth could—and had—run the business singlehandedly, especially in those awful weeks after Graham's death.

"Your date is here."

Grace felt her mouth fall open. She snapped it shut, annoyed at herself. She could not have predicted, after all this preparation, how easy it would be to become flustered.

"My date?" she squeaked and then pulled herself together. "I don't have a date. I have a business appointment."

"Grace, he's gorgeous. I'm thinking Hugh Jackman only a hundred times better. No! No! Tracker Tannison!"

Don't ask. She asked. "Who is Tracker Tannison?"

"The TV series, *Find Your Man.* He plays Special Agent Booth Bentley. He's dreamy. But not as dreamy as your date."

After all her careful preparation, Grace felt as though her head was spinning. She felt a desperate need to get this situation under control.

Aware of a certain tight note, of enunciating every word very carefully, Grace said, "I do not have a date."

"He says it's a date."

"It isn't."

Beth was looking at her closely. "Well, you look like it is."

"I don't. I've worn this suit dozens of times."

"I meant the blush."

"I am not blushing!"

"If you say so." Beth scrutinized her. "Isn't that wool? It's supposed to go to thirty-two degrees Celsius today."

"We have air-conditioning."

"That suit is extremely flattering. I've always loved that color on you," Beth said, soothingly, making Grace aware she was telegraphing her distress at the fact her plan for this meeting already seemed to be going awry. But at least it wasn't eight ponies on the loose, a broken shoe and a smudged dress.

"Make him wait. Until I'm done blushing." *Until I've collected myself.* "Ten minutes. Then show him in."

Those would be the longest ten minutes of her life. A date? How dare he say it was a date?

"He told me to send you out."

Grace allowed herself to feel flabbergasted by the pure arrogance of the man!

"Well, I'm not going out. You tell him to come in. He's not the boss over you. Or me." Oh, God. She sounded exactly like Tucker.

"Grace?"

She closed her eyes. She just knew something terrible was coming. She could feel it, like storm clouds building on the horizon.

"He's got a Ferrari sitting outside the front door. He said he's taking you for a ride."

She closed her eyes. She mustered all her strength, which was what it took to utter one little word.

"No."

"It's red."

"So what?" But her voice had a high, desperate note to it. The truth? She was beginning to wish for ponies!

"Well, I can't help but notice, when you open your wallet, you have that picture..." Beth's voice trailed away. And then stronger, she said, "Go, for God's sake. You might never have this opportunity again. That man is absolutely gorgeous. And even if he was a toad, you should go for a ride in that car."

Grace glared at Beth. Imagine that. The devil looked like her secretary today.

"No," she said.

"If you're going to tell him no, you do it yourself." Beth, loyal secretary and friend turned traitor, gave her a meaningful look and slipped out the door.

Before it shut behind her, Grace heard Beth say, "Can you just give her a moment?"

The door shut.

Now she had to go say no herself. She had to tell him their meeting was going to go just as she planned it, in the safety of her office, where he could admire her decor and her flowers and her outfit. Where she could erase any last vestiges of a woman throwing shoes at a pony. Where she could erase any last vestiges of a woman who needed the prissy look wiped off her face...with his lips.

Still, if she said no, and said it too vehemently, how was he going to read that? At the very least, control freak. At the very worst, fighting a terrible attraction to him. She had to prove to him—no, she had to prove to herself—that Rory Adams had no power over her.

None.

So, she would go out there, and she would not see going to him as any kind of defeat. No, living up to her name, she would do it gracefully. She would still say no, of course, but with no vehemence at all. She would say it with a reluctant smile. She would explain, *I'm just too busy today. A huge wedding coming up this weekend. So much to do.*

She got up. She went to the door. She flung it open. Is this how he had felt going into battle?

His heart pounding in his chest? His palms slicked with sweat?

She wished she hadn't thought of him like that, going

into battle. Because Rory Adams was sitting in a chair, leafing casually through a magazine, a man who, despite his aura of great power, had spent a great deal of his life waiting...for all hell to break loose.

There was something about him that was all warrior, despite the civilized backdrop of her office, despite his casual slacks, despite the sports shirt, despite the hair that was long enough to tickle the back of his collar.

Rory looked up at her, and smiled, and she thought of him threatening to kiss her. And wondered if even that was a distraction, something to keep her from seeing who he really was.

Because just behind the devastating charm of that smile she could see the warrior. And worse, she could detect a faint weariness, strength that had been tested to the point of breaking but that had not broken.

"Good morning, Grace."

Her whole prepared speech about how important and busy she was abandoned her.

This man had been her brother's friend. He was here trying to do something nice for her. Probably to honor her brother.

She could not treat him like the enemy.

Not even to protect herself.

"I hear we're going for a ride," she said. She cast a warning glance at Beth who looked as if she was going to stand up from behind her desk and clap.

"I was hoping you could squeeze it in."

He was offering her an out. It was her last chance to claim, yes, indeed, she was too busy. If she looked away from him, maybe her head would clear.

Maybe she would have a better chance of making the right and rational decision.

Her eyes moved beyond him, but unfortunately they drifted to the big picture window of her office that faced the front street. The car was parked at the curb, already attracting attention. Two teenage boys had their cell phones out and were taking turns taking pictures of each other posing with the car.

For as long as she could remember, Grace had carried a picture of a red Ferrari in her wallet. If you asked her why, she didn't even know. It appealed to some part of her that was deeply secret.

She was not sure how she felt about this secret being exposed to Rory Adams. Her brother must have told him. That link, her brother, connected her to this man in ways she was not at all sure she could handle.

And she liked having a handle on her life!

Instead, Grace felt the terrible loss of control. And she felt an equally terrible temptation just to surrender. She fought it.

"We are going to discuss Warrior Down?" she asked, trying for a stern note, trying to recapture at least an illusion of control.

"Of course," he said smoothly.

"All right. Beth clear my calendar for—" She looked inquiringly at him.

"A couple of hours?"

Impossible. But her control seemed to have abandoned her despite her attempt to fight for it. "All right."

But in one last ditch effort to salvage something of all that time wasted in an effort to manipulate his impressions of her, Grace darted back into her office and grabbed the flowers, hugged them to her chest.

She plunked them down on Beth's desk. "These need water," she said, regally, and Beth, bless her heart, did not say *But they just arrived.*

She said, "Oh, yes, I noticed that. I'll look after it right away."

And before Rory could get a look at the water level in that crystal vase, Grace marched by him, waited for him to open the door for her, and then passed through it, and waited for him to open the door of the car.

The car was red and low and so sexy it took her breath away. It had a hard top that had been retracted.

She hesitated, feeling as if if she did it, if she actually stepped into that car something in her life was going to change irrevocably and forever.

Don't do it.

Do it.

Don't.

Do.

Do was winning. What was so great about her life that it couldn't stand changing? She worked, she slept, she worked some more. She did an important job. She brought people joy. She made happy memories for them.

That's what dedicated career women did: they got their sense of fulfillment from their work. That's what women who didn't want to be hurt anymore did.

Yesterday it had seemed like a perfectly acceptable life, she wailed a reminder to herself.

No, the day before yesterday. Before the ponies. Before him.

The door of the car whispered open. She could smell

the heat of the engine, Italian leather and Rory's cologne.

They were drugs that stole what was left of her resolve. Grace Day took one more step toward the car.

CHAPTER FOUR

"Hang on," Rory said as Grace moved by him to get in the car. She tried not to brush against him but the effort was lost when his hand went to her hair. He ran his palm along the side of her face, over her ear, until it rested on the delicate nape of her neck. With a gentle, firm tug he freed the clasp that held her hair up.

Grace felt her hair tumble, whisper against the sensitive skin of her neck where his fingers had just touched.

How dare you would be the appropriate response. To turn around and march right back into her office, and her perfectly satisfactory life, slam the door and turn the bolt would be the appropriate response.

Instead, she felt the shiver of his touch, of the strange intimacy of him releasing her hair, to the bottom of her toes. Instead, she stood there frozen, captured by the shimmering greenness of his eyes, and by the glint of hard, male appreciation in them.

"You can't ride with the top down without feeling the wind in your hair," he said, something in his voice faintly gruff. He held out the hair clasp to her.

And she took it and slid it into her pocket without one single word of protest!

Maybe another woman could be stronger. But the

combination of the sexy car and the sensuousness of his touch on her hair and her neck rendered Grace helpless. She could not resist the temptation. Taking a deep breath that she let out with a sigh, she put her leg in the car and then sank into the low seat.

Nothing could live up to a fantasy she'd held for so long, she told herself, trying desperately to regain some semblance of her sensible well-ordered life.

But when Rory Adams came around and took the seat beside her, and the engine started with a deep low purr of pure power, and his scent and the smell of leather both filled her nostrils, she had the awful thought that maybe some things could actually be better than a fantasy.

"Where are we going?" Grace asked him.

"Does it matter?" He shoulder-checked and pulled away from the curb so smoothly it was as if she was riding on air.

Whatever was left in her that wanted to be in control evaporated. She laughed. "No."

"I thought we'd take the back road around Lake Okanagan. Stop at the Blue Water Resort and have lunch."

"That resort is where the big fundraiser for Warrior Down is."

"I know."

She pondered that as they surged in and out of traffic, making their way through Mason to the head of the lake road. Did he know everything? Apparently he did. Even about her lifelong dream to ride in a Ferrari.

"Graham must have told you about my secret fascination with this car," she said.

"Is it everything you expected?" he said with a smile that did not distract her. He didn't want to admit he and Graham had discussed her.

"So far, it's more than I expected," she admitted, but got right back on topic. "I have to admit, it makes me uncomfortable thinking about you two discussing me."

"It should." He sent her a sideways look, and waggled his eyebrows, the villain in a movie. Despite the fact he was still trying to distract her, Grace laughed again, and enjoyed the sensation of laughing. Since Graham had died, and then her engagement had blown up in her face, it really seemed like there had not been much to laugh about. She was not unaware of the irony of the fact that she planned joyous, happy occasions for others, but rarely felt those things herself anymore.

"Do tell," she challenged him.

"Okay. I know just about everything about you. I know your favorite color is yellow. And your favorite book is *Anne of Green Gables.* I know you once punched a boy in your class for stealing a kiss."

"Something for you to remember," she said, pretending haughtiness.

"And that you were suspended for it. That's funny. *You* suspended."

"Despite the fact you think you know everything about me, I am not the Goody Two Shoes you think I am."

"Uh-huh." With utter disbelief. "Tell me something about you that would surprise me."

They were taking the exit now and she could see the dark blue waters of Lake Okanagan blinking under the sunlight in the distance.

She didn't just want to surprise him. She found herself wanting to shock him. So, feeling bold, she said, "I've skinny-dipped in this lake."

His laugh was derisive. "Oh, sure. By yourself at midnight."

"It wasn't! It was at a coed party."

"Oh," he said dryly. "Coed. Boys and girls at the same party. And how many beers did you have to have before you went in? I bet you're completely soused on two. And I'll bet it was completely dark and you raced down to the water's edge wrapped in your towel and didn't take it off until the last possible moment. And then you stayed in the water freezing, scared to come out and were in bed sick for a week after."

She stared at him, aghast at how accurate his portrayal of the one racy event of her entire life was. Obviously, he and Graham had talked about her way too much!

"So," he said, satisfied by her fuming silence, "I know just about everything about you, and you, on the other hand, know nothing about me."

But that wasn't exactly true. A memory of his house came to her mind. When he had moved in, the house his family had occupied had been the only rental on their block. Everyone else owned their properties and had been in them for years, forming a family as much as a neighborhood.

And then the Adamses had arrived and moved into a neglected two-story down the street from her own house. The neglect, as she recalled, was not improved by his family's possession.

Outside, paint peeled and fences sagged, and inside

curtains drooped and burnt-out lightbulbs were not replaced. The lawn sprouted weeds, an occasional motorcycle, newspapers tangled in the shrubbery. One old, dilapidated car replaced another in the parking spot in front of that house.

Somehow, even though he had challenged her that she knew nothing about him, Grace could not bring that up. She could not tell him that he was a long, long way from his humble roots.

But he glanced at her face, and she was shocked by what an open book she was to him.

"Oh, wait," he said, slowly. "You do know a thing or two about me. Boy from the wrong side of the tracks."

"You lived on the same block as me!"

For a moment something in his face closed, he became intensely focused on driving the car as they entered the first of the twists in the road that ran in a serpentine around this edge of the lake. When he finally glanced at her, a small grin was on his face. "Don't kid yourself, Gracie-Facie. Same block, different worlds. The Cleavers meet the Osbornes. Only, the poor version."

The grin was a fake. It said it didn't matter. It said it didn't bother him, but there was something guarded in his eyes, daring her to judge him.

She wanted to tell him it didn't matter, but she remembered all too clearly the police cars arriving on their quiet street, the shouting from inside their house, a rather memorable occasion when his mother had stumbled out onto the street drinking straight from a wine bottle.

And she remembered the dignity with which he had

handled that, the pride flashing in his eyes as he had retrieved his mother from in front of all her neighbors, walked her back into the house with straight shoulders, his hand on his mother's elbow, never glancing back at the assembled neighbors.

"You know something about growing up in a house like that, Gracie?"

She knew he was trusting her with something, and that this was not something he did often. The grin was completely gone.

"When you grow up in a war zone, you never expect anything good from life. That bred-into-the-bone cynicism made me a born soldier. And it always made me feel I had a leg up on those who did expect good things."

She had to admit, he had something there. Look at her, going through life like Pollyanna, her dreams broken at every turn!

But still, there was something about him not expecting good things that made her sad.

"When you expect the worst," he said, his voice grim, "you are rarely disappointed."

"And what happens when the best happens?" she asked. "What happens when the boy from the wrong side of the tracks ends up in the red Ferrari?"

"Don't forget the part about the girl next door being with him," he added, and the grin was back, devil-may-care, daring her to see beyond it. The thing was, she *could* see beyond it.

"I'm being serious!"

"Are you ever anything else?"

"Occasionally! But not now. What do you feel when the best happens instead of the worst?"

"Oh, that word again. *Feel.*"

"As uncomfortable as it makes you, could you answer the question?"

"When good things happen, I enjoy every second of them. Without any expectation that it will last."

He was telling her something, and she was aware she needed to pay attention. He wasn't the staying kind. He wasn't the lasting kind.

And what did she care? She would never think of Rory Adams like that.

Only, a secret part of her always had. And she was suddenly aware that secret part probably always would.

He would be such a foolish choice to fall for.

But he was right. She was being way too serious. She reminded herself it wasn't in her new life agenda to fall for anyone. The exact opposite, in fact.

Besides, Rory hadn't proposed they spend their lives together. He was giving her a day. And a dream.

And even if he was maintaining his own cynicism, she just needed to enjoy it, for this to be her *occasionally,* for this to be the day when she was not so serious.

When was the last time she had just had fun? A carefree day? A long, long time ago, certainly not since her brother had died.

She was accepting this as the unexpected gift it was. She was not even allowing herself to think that there might be a price to pay later.

"Rory?"

"Um?"

"Could you go a wee bit faster?"

He laughed and complied and she felt the thrill of both things: his laughter and the adrenaline of moving fast, a little closer to the edge. And Grace was aware his laughter brought that as surely as the power of the car did.

"Tell me about the car," she called over the roar of the engine and the wind in her hair.

"This is a 2011 Ferrari, a 458 Spider with a V8 rear engine."

"Somehow I don't think they rent these to just anybody," she guessed dryly. "In fact, where do you rent a car like this in Mason?"

"It's not exactly from Mason," he said, a little uncomfortably. "I had to make special arrangements to get it."

"First cowboys and now a Ferrari. If I ever need a rabbit pulled out of a hat, I guess you're my go-to guy, hmm?"

"If you ever need anything, Gracie," he said quietly, "I'm your go-to guy."

The simple statement, said so matter-of-factly, made her turn her face away from him so he could not see how deeply it affected her.

He was a man who said what he meant and meant what he said. And those simple words—that promise she could have someone to count on—filled her with unexpected emotion.

Dumb, since after Harold she had been so resolute in her intention not to rely on anyone for anything. Her plan now was to be one of those independent women who scoffed at *need*. She would hang her own pictures and refinish her own floors. When she came across a project she couldn't do, she would hire someone.

After Harold, she had been resolute in her intention

not just to be independent physically but also to be that way emotionally. Not to rely on anyone to make her feel anything anymore, and so the emotion clawing at her throat and stinging at her eyes because of his simple words, *I'm your go-to guy* felt as if it could swamp her whole plan for her life!

But riding in the car was a much-appreciated distraction from the unexpected meeting with her own secret longings, and she made herself focus on that. She might never, after all, experience something like this again!

She took off her jacket and threw it behind her seat.

And, after a while, she allowed herself to appreciate these moments with Rory. She liked the way one of his hands rested, light and confident on the wheel, the other on the gear shift. She liked the look on his face, relaxed but alert. Ready.

And she liked the way he drove. Many men would have gone crazy driving a car like this, but Rory drove without aggression, playing with the power but not unleashing it totally. It was as if he was riding a high-strung horse and he was in perfect control.

He put a CD in and the raspy tones of an old rock-and-roll band that had stood the test of time and could still fill stadiums filled the car.

The choice of music. The way he drove. The house he had come from. *If you ever need anything, Gracie, I'm your go-to guy.* How could he think she did not know anything about him?

She leaned back into her seat, felt the wind play with her hair. And surrendered.

* * *

Rory sat across the white linen tablecloth and watched Grace. The view of the lake from where they sat on the marble outdoor terrace of the Blue Water Resort's restaurant was amazing. Grace had already told him, her eyes sparking with excitement, the transformations she planned for this space when the Warrior Down fundraiser was to be held here in the last days of August.

He had talked her into a glass of wine from a local winery, while refusing one himself.

"You're not going to have one?" she asked.

"No. You don't drive a car that powerful and that sensitive with anything in your system that could impair your judgment."

He could tell she liked that, that his attention to safety appealed to her.

But there was a deeper truth behind his refusal to join her for a drink—and it wasn't just that he wanted to prove himself right that she would be soused on two.

He had long ago come to rely on his instincts. There were times his survival and the survival of others had depended on that. Now, he rarely ever did anything that made those instincts fuzzy. He had not had a drink in at least five years.

Was it just about his instincts being muddied? Or was part of it about his family's history with alcohol, trying to divorce himself from that completely?

And he was acutely aware there was already something about being with her that had impaired his judgment.

He didn't talk about his family, *ever,* and he tried not to think about them. What had made him bring it up? Just the fact she already knew? The fact she had grown up just down the street from the ongoing circus that had been his family life?

No. More than that.

He had trusted her with something about himself he did not trust everyone with.

"What happened to your fiancé?" he asked. For a guy who prided himself on his instincts, it was probably the wrong question. The door of camaraderie that had been opening between them snapped shut.

Or maybe that was exactly what he wanted to happen.

"What do you know about my fiancé?" she asked warily.

"Graham talked about your engagement when it happened. He didn't much care for, um, Herbert."

"Harold."

"So, what happened?"

She was so silent that for a moment he thought she wasn't going to tell him. She looked out at the lake, where children were playing on a float. Pushing each other off it, their splashing and laughter shivering on the air.

But when she looked back at him, he saw she was struggling to contain her emotion.

He was not good with emotion.

He wished he hadn't opened this kettle of fish. That door of camaraderie that had squeaked shut, was suddenly flung open, wider than before.

"He left me," she said bravely, tilting her chin up as if she didn't care. Her eyes told a completely different story, and he was aware he was seeing Gracie at her most real and her most raw.

And that she was trusting him with that.

Just as he had trusted her.

He waited.

"He left me because he couldn't stand the grief. He said it was time to get over it. He said it was time to be who I was before."

Rory felt a ripple of pure fury that he was very careful not to show her. In fact, his voice was very measured when he spoke. "Gracie?"

She looked at her hands.

"He was wrong. You never get over it. You're never who you were before."

She looked up at him, and the gratitude in her eyes was so intense it shook him. But he understood then, that the death of Graham was a bond between them. Unbreakable. They, alone, understood what it was to lose a man like that, how it changed the world forever for the worse.

"I hope I never meet old Herbert," he said, getting the name wrong deliberately, letting her know the name was not important. The character of a man was important.

"Why is that?" she asked.

"Because I won't be responsible for what happens next."

He thought she would reprimand him for his insinuated violence. Maybe he even hoped for it: to close that open door again. That something about showing her this little flash of who he *really* was, how quickly he could go to the dark side, would frighten her just a little bit.

He was not sure he was ready for her trust.

Yes, she could rely on him to be her go-to guy; no,

she could not rely on him to handle things her way, which would be all sweetness and light.

He was aware, again, of having darkness in him that could snuff her light.

But instead of her seeing that, instead of her being properly wary of him, she said, ever so softly, "Thank you."

Still, the intensity of that moment must have shaken her nearly as badly as it shook him: how fiercely protective he felt of her, how joined to her.

Grace changed the subject abruptly. "Tell me about your business, and what you'd like to do for Warrior Down."

Or maybe it was the most natural of segues, thoughts of her brother turning to ways that they could both honor his memory.

Rory was more an action guy than a talker, so it surprised him how easily he opened up to her.

"When I first enlisted, my brother, Sam, was just getting out of high school. He was a really talented artist and he wanted to get into graphics. I didn't have much to spend my money on, so I invested in him. In his education, later in his idea for a company.

"He got his big break doing graphics on a car for Saul Bellissimo. Do you know that name?"

"A race-car driver?" she ventured.

"*The* race-car driver of the past few years. Anyway, he did Saul's car, and that got him all kinds of other jobs and publicity. Sam just kept pushing the envelope, first graphic wraps for race cars, then he got the contract to do some buses.

"He's an artist, and to everyone's surprise I'm good at business."

"I'm not surprised," she said. "Tell me more."

It was another moment where something shivered along Rory's spine. It was as if Grace saw things in him that others didn't. And her interest in him was genuine. He should not allow himself to be flattered, but he did.

"Because of good access to the internet most of the time, I could even keep involved while I was overseas. When I decided to leave the service, I was a little astonished to find myself the CEO of a pretty viable company. In the past couple of months we completed our first contract for an airline company, graphic-wrapping their planes. In the next month or so, we're going to do our first graphic wrap on a building."

"A building?" she said. "Where?"

"Melbourne, Australia."

"My goodness, Rory, you're an international mogul!"

He felt the danger zone he was in. Boy from the wrong side of the tracks basking in the admiration of the wholesome girl from next door.

Enjoying her admiration in no way meant it was going any further.

He scrambled to keep it impersonal. "It all puts us in a pretty good position to sponsor something for Warrior Down."

"What did you have in mind?"

"I went on the internet and looked at your outline for the event. It sounds great. Dinner. Dance. Silent auction, everything set up here on the edge of the lake. I thought we might contribute something to the silent auction."

"Like?"

"What if we thought outside the box? Something like 'A Perfect Day.' A helicopter ride to the top of a mountain for a champagne lunch, something like that? Or maybe a ride in Saul's car, a turn or two around the track. Or maybe both."

"That's fantastic."

It was wrong to be so darned pleased that she was so darned pleased. It was wrong to want to bask in her admiration all afternoon. Still, a man was allowed a few weaknesses, wasn't he?

"What's your perfect day?" he asked her. "Because we could do anything—an elephant ride in Thailand, bungee-jumping... Literally if you can think of it, we can do it."

Now he was just showing off, plain and simple. He thought he'd better buy Bridey some flowers tomorrow, since she'd be the one executing whatever scheme they came up with.

"Oh." Grace looked flustered. "I thought I was a bit of an expert on perfect days, but my mind doesn't even begin to work like that. Elephants in Thailand?"

"Just close your eyes, then, and tell me what comes. Your perfect day."

And suddenly he wanted to know very, very badly, because it seemed like it would tell him secret things about her.

"Nothing so grand as elephants or helicopters," she said tentatively, not closing her eyes, but taking a forti-fying sip of her wine before she bared her soul to him. She gazed out at the water, and then said, "You see those kids playing over there? Swimming out to the float and jumping in the water? That looks darn near perfect to me."

It had become quite hot in the last hour. Her blouse was sticking to her in the nicest places, and the skirt, which was about the most flattering straitlaced outfit he had ever seen, seemed to be causing her grief. He probably should not have suggested lunch outside.

He'd given her a chance to choose anything, and she had chosen that? It did tell him just about everything about her.

Except for her one Ferrari fantasy, she was just as she seemed. Wholesome. Without airs. Why did that seem kind of refreshing instead of just boring?

"That's too easy for a perfect day," he chided her. "We could have that today."

"I've already had days like that," she said, a little wistfully. "We used to have the cottage on Mara Lake. Not the multimillion-dollar kind you see today. A real cottage—ramshackle, falling down, no power, an outhouse. And all I remember there are perfect endless summer days."

"I remember your family heading out to that cottage, your station wagon packed to the roof." He did not say anything about that funny little twist of envy he would feel when he watched them depart, the longing to be part of something like that.

And, oddly, at the same time he had longed for it, he had refused every invitation Graham had offered him to join them there.

He'd felt as if he had to resist ever tasting something he knew he could not have.

People from perfect families matched up with other

people from perfect families. He had known that before he'd gone away to war and become even more hard and more cynical than he had been back then, and that had been plenty hard and cynical for a kid.

It suddenly seemed that this was a demon he needed to face: punch a hole in that illusion of a perfect life or a perfect day.

"Let's have it today," he said. "We'll put on some swimsuits and jump in the lake before we go home."

And he would find the wholesomeness of it hokey and boring, and somehow break free of the spell she was weaving around him.

"No. It's perfectly all right. I've already had a perfect day. Thank you for the car. It really was an incredibly sweet thing to do."

"Ah, I'm a sweet guy," he said, and wagged his eyebrows at her fiendishly.

But she didn't buy it. "What *do* you think you are?"

He could distract her with charm. Why ruin a light moment? But something overtook him, had been overtaking him ever since he remembered the perfect Day family leaving for their cottage, had been overtaking him ever since he had seen her again herding the damn ponies.

It was as though he was driven to show her what was real about him, driven to see if she could handle it.

It was the perfect time to tell her how he had failed her brother, but somehow he was not ready for that.

"Who I really am? Cynical. Dark. Aggressive when the situation calls for it."

He hated that he had said that. It made him feel as vulnerable as if he had told her the whole truth about her brother. He had exposed a wound to her that he had succeeded in hiding from the whole world. And so he finished with just a touch of sarcasm, "In other words, Gracie, not your type. At all."

As he had hoped, she was insulted. "Whoever said you were my type?" she said with a bit of heat.

"No one. Just to keep you from getting ideas."

"I would not ever get an idea about you!"

"Great. Let's go swimming before you sweat to death in the skirt you didn't put on for me."

"I don't have a bathing suit." Her voice was stiff with indignation. So, she *had* picked out that delectable, sexy and too warm suit just for him.

"Is that wool?" he said leaning over the table to get a better look. It was sticking to her, and she tugged it away.

"Very lightweight wool," she said, annoyed. "We should leave now."

"We should go swimming. What are you afraid of?"

"I'm not afraid of anything! I just don't happen to carry a bathing suit in my purse. Though I'm sure *your type* would."

"And what is my type, Gracie?"

"Bimbo," she said, without any hesitation at all.

He lifted his water glass to her. "Touché."

She gulped back the rest of her wine. Her cheeks had pretty red spots on them. He was right. One glass and she was practically soused.

She tossed the glossy wave of auburn hair that he had been dumb enough to set free, looked him straight in the face and said, "There are all kinds of stores here at the resort. I guess I could find a bathing suit."

He could tell it was not in her plan for the day, and that it did not come naturally to her to be spontaneous.

And maybe spontaneity between them had some dangerous overtones, given the startling intensity that had unfolded between them.

She wanted to move away from it.

And so did he.

And at the same time, he wanted to see if he could be immune to her. If he could burst the myth that he had always had surrounding her family.

He supposed she'd buy a one-piece suit, about as sexy as the uniforms of the East German girls' swim team, pre-Wall collapse.

And even though that was exactly what he wanted, he goaded her.

"When you buy that bathing suit? Be the girl in the red Ferrari," he suggested, "not an old stick-in-the mud."

Instead of looking offended, she looked suddenly sad. "Graham used to accuse me of that."

"I know," he said softly. "Break loose, Gracie."

And then he wondered what the hell he was playing with, and why. He looked after the check, and they separated in search of swimwear. He purchased a pair of trunks from one of the hotel stores in about two seconds, left them on, and went and sat on a bench where she would see him when she came out of the store she was in.

He had turned off his phone just before picking Grace up this morning, and now he turned it back on and sorted through his incoming messages.

Only one interested him. From Slim McKenzie, the cowboy who had accompanied Serenity home.

Rory glanced toward the store. Through a plate-glass window he could see Gracie holding up a very Gracie bathing suit. It probably had a matching bathing cap with a flower over one ear.

He listened to Slim's message and taking one more glance at the window to make sure Gracie would not materialize while he was in the middle of the call, he called back.

"Sorry, Mr. Adams. The kid tossed the soda can out the window before I could grab it."

"Never heard of littering?" Rory asked.

There was a pause. "Littering? I think that kid would laugh at the concept that that was a bad thing to do. He's pretty streetwise. Anyway, they were camped in an area off Bixby Road about six kilometers this side of Grumbly. The property was clearly marked No Trespassing. I don't think they had permission to be there. There was a creek to water the horses, but I didn't see much in the way of grass, and I didn't see any hay."

"The ponies looked fat to me."

"Yeah. Unfortunately, horses who aren't on a proper parasite-control program can look fat. That's called worm belly. Also from eating poor-quality feed. That's called hay belly."

"You're telling me the horses were hungry." Or full of worms. Way more than he'd ever wanted to know about an equine's belly.

"I think they were hungry. That's why they broke loose at the park and were so hard to catch."

Rory did not want to get involved in this. And yet how could he not be involved? If the horses were hungry, chances were the kid was, too.

He hung up the phone, frowning, and not just because his soda-pop-can plan had failed, either. He glanced at the window. Grace had disappeared from sight.

He could just call the authorities. There were people whose job it was to look after things like this and he was not one of those people. But even though he couldn't see Gracie, it seemed like just being around her required him to be a better man.

He sighed and called Bridey.

"Mr. Adams, *sir.*"

"I need some good-quality hay delivered to some ponies. And a couple of days' worth of groceries for a kid and his mom. I need you to track down a landowner and get permission to use his land. Offer him whatever it takes to get that permission. You can use Slim again to deliver the food and the hay. He knows the situation and the location."

He hung up and glanced again at the window. Gracie was back in view, wearing a huge white robe, and peering at a rack of bathing suits as if it were the enemy. Her tongue, as she flipped rapidly through hangers, was caught between her teeth in fierce concentration. Obviously she was torn between being a stick-in-the-mud and shocking the hell out of him.

He hoped she would be a stick-in-the-mud and at the same time he didn't hope that at all. He was not used to being a man divided. He was used to being a man who knew exactly what he wanted.

Rory sighed, aware he did not want Gracie Day to know anything that he had just found out about Tucker and Serenity. If ever there would be a sucker for starving ponies, it would be her. Throw in the kid and that remote possibility that Tucker was Graham's, and she'd be mortgaging her business to save them.

He had no choice. He had to protect her. And the catch? She could never know he was protecting her.

Break loose, Gracie.

Those words echoed in Gracie's head as she studied the bathing-suit rack. How could a girl back down from a challenge like that? How could any woman in the world not rise to the bait? She *needed* to show him he had it all wrong.

That she was no stick-in-the-mud.

She selected a navy-blue tank-style, planning to defy his instruction to break loose. She held it up, studied it, silently declared it perfect. The matching bathing cap, with its huge plastic rose over the ear was a little silly, but the bathing suit would definitely do.

Except that it wouldn't. As soon as Grace took it to the change room and tried it on, she knew it was all wrong. The bathing suit, on, while definitely practical, made her look about as sexy as a refrigerator box. Just the kind of suit a stick-in-the mud would choose in a pinch!

So, going way out of her comfort zone, she wrapped herself in the robe provided by the shop and peeked out of the change room.

She could see Rory sitting on a bench on the open-air walkway, talking on his cell phone, comfortable in his new swim trunks, looking at the lake.

Life was so unfair sometimes! When a guy needed a bathing suit, he just went and grabbed one off the rack and put it on. There was no twisting and turning and looking at it from this angle and that, no self-doubt, no feelings of not being perfect!

While she watched, he hung up the phone, put it back in his pocket. He gazed out over the lake, and she was taken by his stillness while he waited, a man who had learned to appreciate quiet moments—that lull before the storm—when he could get them.

What he wasn't expecting was that she—little Gracie-Facie Day—was going to be his storm!

She looked back at the rack of suits, and this time refused even to look at the huge offering of one-piece suits. Taking a deep breath, she picked a half dozen of the skimpiest she could find!

A few moments later, she stared at herself in the change-room mirror.

Somehow, without planning it, maybe even against her will, she had become a totally different woman from the one who had walked into her office this morning.

"Not too late to put on the blue tank," she whispered to herself.

But she knew she wasn't going to.

CHAPTER FIVE

"My, my," Rory said, rising to join her as she came out of the shop, "Could you have found a bigger towel?"

He looked wickedly amused and Grace realized the huge towel she had purchased to wrap herself in only confirmed what he had suspected earlier when she had shared her skinny-dipping experience with him.

Goody Two Shoes. She was in a no-win position. If she dropped the towel now, she would feel like an idiot, displaying herself to him. If she didn't, she would feel like the prude he so clearly thought she was!

"My skin is sensitive to the sun," she said. "I haven't been on the beach yet this year." Shouldering her freshly purchased beach bag with her turquoise suit crumpled up inside it, she moved by him onto the flagstone pathway that wound down to the beach.

"You're going to have to take it off sometime," he said. "I wonder what you have on underneath it?"

She wished fervently for the blue suit that she had hung back up with a certain pride in the new her. She was not feeling nearly so bold now. In fact, she was feeling well out of her league.

"I have on the kind of suit a girl who rides in a

Ferrari would wear," she said with as much sophistication as she could muster.

"Ah, here's the rub, my Gracie, the girl in the Ferrari wouldn't have bothered with the towel."

My Gracie?

"Unless she burned easily," she retorted stubbornly.

"Tanning beds have a way of eliminating that problem."

"Hasn't your fictional Ferrari girl ever heard of melanoma?"

"Mel-a-nom-a. Is that three syllables?"

"Four."

He laughed. "That would be a no, then."

"Bimbo."

"Touché," he said, and somehow she found herself smiling.

They reached the hotel beach and she shuffled through the hot sand to the water's edge.

"Not going to lie in the sun and heat up a little first?" he asked smoothly.

She decided not to share with him that the wool suit she had so foolishly worn for precisely the reason he had guessed had heated her up quite enough for one day.

Sending him a little sidelong glance, she unhooked the towel from where it was clamped under her armpits. Unnerved by his frank anticipation of the towel dropping, Grace plunged into the water before the towel was even done slithering to the ground.

She couldn't help the little shriek at the cold, but still she did not stop until the water was up to her neck.

"Come in," she said. "It's beautiful."

"Liar. Your teeth are chattering."

"Chicken."

His eyes narrowed. "No one calls me a chicken and gets away with it, Gracie."

"Bok-bok-bok-bok-bok."

He hit the water running, dived cleanly, was nearly at her in one powerful stroke.

But she had grown up swimming and playing in these ice-cold waters, and she turned quickly from him and swam with expert strokes for the float.

She made it to the float a breath ahead of him, and clung to the side, scared if she got out of the water, the bathing suit might not come with her.

"Some suits," he growled in her ear, "are not exactly designed for swimming are they, Gracie?"

She pulled an errant strap back on her shoulder. This was turning into a repeat of yesterday!

He began to hum *Itsy Bitsy Teeny Weeny Yellow Polka-Dot Bikini.* Deliberately defiant, trying to find a red Ferrari girl in herself somewhere, Gracie hauled herself up, thankful the children who had been there earlier had departed and did not catch a glimpse of all the parts of her slipping from her suit. She quickly adjusted and then turned back to face him.

He was laughing so hard he was having trouble treading water. That was not exactly the effect she had intended.

"I'm coming to get you, Gracie. Nobody calls me a chicken." He switched from his *Yellow Polka-Dot Bikini* humming to a much more sinister tune, which she recognized as the theme music from *Jaws.*

Then he launched himself at the float. When he tried to pull himself up on the water-grayed wooden planks, she waited until he was precariously balanced on his forearms, placed all her weight on his shoulders and shoved.

He fell back in the water with a splash, and she barely had time to register how lovely his shoulders, skin and muscle had felt under her touch. She bounced on the balls of her feet, waiting for his next attempt.

He trod water for a moment, and she became aware he wasn't laughing now. She fought the urge to cover herself. With what, after all? Why not just enjoy the gleaming appreciation in his eyes? Why not play with it? Why not be the fun and flirtatious kind of girl who would wear a suit like this and ride in a red Ferrari?

"I'm giving you one chance to surrender," he told her.

"No. I hold the high ground and I intend to keep it."

"Ha. You haven't a hope, Gracie-Facie."

"Maybe you haven't a hope."

He came again, lifted himself up. She placed her foot solidly on the slickness of his wet chest and pushed. He fell back again, but this time he grabbed at her ankle and she slid forward before shaking free.

He came again, and this time she went for his head. She leaned out precariously, shoved and he went under the water easily.

Too easily, because just as she was congratulating herself on repelling another attack, a hand snaked out of the water and locked on her wrist. He tugged and she flew off the float and over his head, landing with an ungracious splash.

Now he clambered up on the float, and repelled her efforts to get up on it. Soon, the air was shimmering with their shouts and their laughter.

She forgot to be self-conscious. She just became immersed in the playful sensuality of the moment: cold water, wet bodies, a perfect summer day and a perfect man to enjoy it with.

She finally managed to get her hands locked around one of his knees and refused to let go, hanging on like a terrier to a bull.

He plunged into the water beside her. Surfaced, shaking droplets of water from his hair, shouting with laughter.

"Okay," he said, finally, when they were both gasping for air, breathless from laughing, as sodden as half-drowned puppies. "You've worn me out. I'll share the float with you."

"May I count that as a surrender?"

"You may count it as a truce."

She pretended to be thinking about it. "All right."

He pulled himself up on the float, held his arm out and she took it. He yanked her from the water with amazing strength, and they stood there in the bright sun, dripping water and staring at each other, something as sizzling as the sun in the air between them.

Rory Adams was as perfect as God had ever made a man. His features were chiseled, masculine, glorious. His muscles, beaded with water, told a story of easy, self-assured strength. And his eyes were the most intense shade of green she had ever seen.

His gaze moved with frank appreciation to where the water slid from her hair down in between the minute protection of the two tiny scraps of fabric that hid her breasts.

And then they moved to her lips.

And for a moment, while they rested there, she felt the heat of it, wanted what he wanted.

But then he turned, flopped down on the deck and patted the worn boards beside him.

She flopped down and felt the delicious heat of the sun on her cold skin.

"How come you never came home, Rory? Graham came when he could. For Christmas at the very least."

He was silent, she sensed debating how much of himself to trust her with. And she felt a little thrill when he spoke, knowing intuitively she had passed a test not many had passed.

"I was so glad to get out of my house that, except for my brother, I never looked back. The military was heaven for me. Routines, rules. Meals."

"You could have come home with Graham. I know he asked you."

"I tried to spend holidays with my brother. We both liked to pretend it wasn't Christmas at all. We went skiing, sometimes. California, once. France, another time."

Despite the fact he tossed that out casually, she hurt for him. "How are your parents, Rory? They moved out of the neighborhood shortly after you left."

"They're both gone. My mom first, cirrhosis, my dad a few years later in an accident."

"I didn't know," she said. "Graham never said anything."

"They lived hard. People who live like that die young."

She scanned his face. It was closed.

"I'm sorry," she said. Not for the deaths of his parents, but for him. For growing up like that, for the loneliness of having nowhere to go at Christmas, for being so alone in the world he had not shared his pain with his best friend.

He closed his eyes. For a moment, she thought he had shut down completely.

"How are your parents, Grace?"

He obviously wanted to move on. She could tell he did not like it that he had revealed so much of himself to her.

But she felt deeply honored by his trust. And somehow, despite the fact she was nearly naked beside the most glorious man in the world, it suddenly felt easy to be with him. In so many ways it was as if he was brand-new to her, but there was also a sense of knowing him. He had been in and out of her house with her brother for a couple of years.

She told him about her parents, and then ventured into the territory of old haunts: the park at the end of the street where she'd caught him and Graham smoking cigarettes and threatened to tell.

"You were a sanctimonious little brat."

The high school and mutual acquaintances, what childhood sweethearts had married and who was now divorced. He closed his eyes and it gave her a chance to study him, to breathe in the just-out-of-the-water purity of his skin, to marvel at the thick ropes of his hair where they touched the broad perfection of his shoulders.

When she had gotten up this morning, could she have predicted a day like this? When was the last time she had allowed herself to be surprised? When had she developed this death grip on life, feeling as if she ever let go of control things would spiral wildly toward chaos and destruction?

The sun dried the water on their skin, and she became aware of how good she felt. Relaxed. Did she dare say happy?

Yes, happy.

"I'm happy," she said it out loud, with the wonder it deserved.

"I'm glad," he said, and he opened one eye and looked at her.

"Are you?"

He closed his eye again, seemed to feel the rough boards of the float under the roughening whiskers of his face, seemed to contemplate the question with a deep seriousness.

He opened his eyes and stared at her, and the surprise showed in his eyes and then ran in a grin across the beautiful curve of his mouth.

A real grin, a grin that lit the darkness of his eyes like sun being filtered through a glass pot of steeping tea.

"Yeah," he said, "I am."

"It's been a long time since I felt happy," she admitted.

He was silent. She was aware of his dark eyes on her, aware that something in him was guarded, was aware of it giving way.

"Me, too," he said slowly.

And again some delicious tension built between them. He reached out and traced a drop of water that fell from the thickness of her hair, trickled down the curve of her face to her neck.

He's going to kiss me, she thought.

* * *

I'm going to kiss her, Rory thought with amazement.

Being with her was amazing. What was it about her that made him feel powerless over what was going to happen next?

He didn't talk about his family. And yet he had. And instead of feeling as if he should have kept his mouth shut, he felt unburdened.

Accepted.

And so his sense of amazement increased as his hand traced the droplet of water down her neck, felt how delicate her skin was, possibly the softest thing he had ever felt.

He leaned toward her. He could smell the water on her skin and feel the temperature of her skin changing as it heated under the sun.

Happy.

The thing about happiness for him? It had always felt like a challenge to the gods, something that could be taken away with remarkable swiftness.

He had never gone for Christmas at the Day house because he had known how it would be. Happiness. Closeness.

Him on the outside, looking in, knowing he couldn't have what they had.

He pulled back from the temptation to taste her, looked into her eyes, saw the light, that miraculous light that seemed able to pierce all his shields, that seemed to be able to reach right inside him and pierce the darkness, too.

Having allowed her to make him happy made him feel vulnerable. Open. If you opened yourself to happiness, what other feelings slipped in? He didn't want to be open.

He carried too much with him that he didn't want to let out of the bag. He had lives on his head. From both sides. Brothers who haunted his dreams. Men he called enemy, but that did not make doing what had to be done in any way easier.

He had formed an attitude of survival that involved no attachments.

Except to Graham.

He could not kiss Graham's sister. Or maybe he could. That's what happiness did. It was like wine. It impaired a man's judgment.

A splash broke just off the edge of the float, and there was enough warrior left in him that he was annoyed with himself for not having noticed the approach of the boys.

This was the second time with her that his guard had been broached—yesterday Tucker had caught him off guard.

Today it was young men, teenagers, maybe sixteen or seventeen, three of them.

They hauled themselves up on the float, and began a rambunctious shoving match that was punctuated with some very foul language.

Was he faintly relieved to be exchanging one kind of intensity for a much more familiar kind?

In one move, lithe and silent, Rory found his feet. He crossed his arms over his chest, placed his feet wide, *presence* was second nature to him.

"Enough of the language," he said quietly. He said

nothing else. They could clearly see there was a woman here. He wouldn't point that out to them.

For a moment he saw all the things he'd seen too many times before: boys on the cusp of becoming men, thinking of challenging him. Their expressions were momentarily belligerent, sullen. There was a moment, right here, that he felt, wearily, he had visited a thousand times.

Two teenage boys. Something about them.

It was that microsecond of decision when a bright day could suddenly be marred by darkness. Rory was aware of being completely relaxed, and completely alert at the same time, like a large, predatory cat. He altered his stance only slightly, ready.

The boys saw it. He had sculpted boys their age into men, that he had then sent to die, and they read that history in his stance and his eyes as if he had spoken it out loud. The belligerence fell away.

They mumbled apologies and in a flash had slipped into the water and were gone.

But even so, the magic was completely gone from the day. This was what he carried inside him.

Grace in her world of perfect Christmases and planning birthday parties, did not need it.

Gone, too, was the moment when that kiss had shivered in the air between him and Grace. When he looked at her, he was aware there would be no returning to it. He was not so sure if he saw that as a blessing or a curse.

Grace's eyes were on his face, and he knew she had seen precisely what those boys had seen.

History. Mess with me at your own risk.

Looking at her, suddenly self-conscious again of her

skimpy bathing suit, he was very aware it was not what she needed out of life. Grace Day did not need someone like him.

No, she needed someone solid and dull, who would give her afternoons like this one unmarred by the shadows of what they had seen and who they had become.

Not that being with her and playing in the water had been as dull as he had hoped it would be.

No, instead it had been pure. He had been refreshed. He had felt carefree and young.

It had given him a moment of purity, connection, happiness that he had not experienced for a very long time.

And then those boys had come along and reminded him that this kind of life belonged to someone else.

Rory was aware of needing to get away from her. From the sunny perfection of the day, from her wholesomeness.

From the feeling in his chest—what was that feeling? *A heart heavy with yearning.*

The thought astounded him. He eyed the water, looking for escape from the unexpectedness of that thought.

"You didn't have to do that," she said.

That's where she was wrong. "Yeah," he said. "I did."

"I don't need you to protect me," she said. "I would have told them myself if they were bothering me."

"Right." She could have handled it, just like she was handling Serenity.

He felt himself drawing away from her, forming another plan. He suddenly didn't like the way Grace made him feel.

As if he could tell her anything. Worse, as if he wanted to.

After he dropped her off, he'd head out to that land Serenity had set up camp on. He'd ask her point-blank what she was doing, demand answers, a DNA sample.

Bridey could look after his contribution to Warrior Down. On the way home he would confirm with Grace that his company would provide the perfect day—of her choosing—for silent auction.

And then, with relief, he would turn over the details of making that happen to Bridey. She could do a better job on it than him anyway.

Their roads—his and Grace's—could part right here. He had a million ways to deal with the astonishing discovery of the yearnings he harbored without involving her.

Melbourne, Australia, seemed to be calling his name.

He looked at her, her flawless skin, the bathing suit showing off her perfect womanly curves, the wide eyes, the tangle of her wet hair, the droplets of water pebbled on her skin.

He wondered if Melbourne was going to be far enough away.

"It's getting late," he said. "We'd better go."

He didn't like the way she was looking at him. As if she could see everything about him that he didn't want anyone to see.

What she didn't seem to be seeing? That he would never be worthy of a day like this or a girl like her.

The drive back was sadly silent. He answered her questions with monosyllables. Pulling away. Saving her. Protecting her.

From him.

Finally they pulled up in front of her now-darkened office windows. He got out of the car, held open her door for her.

She didn't hurry by him as he had hoped.

"Thank you," she said.

"Sure."

"We didn't talk much about Warrior Down."

"Just let me know what you consider a perfect day." He gave her a business card. "Call me at this number, and I'll make it happen."

"There couldn't be a more perfect day than the one I just had."

He wasn't getting sucked into her gratitude. He wasn't even going to look at the warmth spilling out of her eyes. Why couldn't she respect the fact he was pulling away for the good of both of them?

"Well, try and think of something that someone might part with a few thousand dollars for. Helicopters. Yachts. Caviar. You know."

And even though she dealt with what people thought was the perfect day all the time, aggravatingly, she did not look like she knew.

Then she did what he least expected. She refused to accept that distance he was trying to put between them.

She reached up, stood on the tips of her toes. Her hair was dry now, but it had dried in a rumpled pile of curls that made him want to touch it. She had put on her uptight suit again, but it was rumpled to the point of ruination, and it didn't hide the woman she had been on that float.

He thought he had never seen a more beautiful

woman. And maybe that's what made him helpless to pull away from her, to do what needed to be done.

He saw it coming. He could see it coming from a mile away. Her half-closed eyes, her deeply inhaled breath, the bow of her mouth drawing into the most adorable little pucker.

He had plenty of time to get away.

But he didn't. He let her.

He let Gracie Day kiss him.

And it was everything he knew it would be. Her lips touching his contained a sweetness he had never known, a delicious innocence.

But when her kiss deepened he detected something else in there. Her hidden Ferrari dreams, her passion, the place in her that old Herbert or Hoover or whatever the hell his name had been would have killed for good.

He pulled back from her, touched his index finger to her chin.

He fought the temptation to take her lips again, to tangle his hands in her hair, to pull her to him, to coax her wild side to the surface.

He'd done hard things his entire life. But nothing quite as hard as walking away from Gracie.

"Don't settle," he said.

"What does that mean?"

It meant not to settle for someone boring and stupid like Harold. But he didn't say that. He said, "It means get rid of that gas-guzzling old-people car you are driving and get something a little spiffy. Don't settle for anything less than your dreams."

Rather than looking appreciative of his advice, she

looked annoyed. A good note to leave her on. He went to turn away.

And stopped. Something caught his attention, something not quite right. In the darkness of her door stoop a paper was fluttering on the window of her office.

Cars parked where they shouldn't be. Teenage boys with a certain look on their faces. Papers fluttering on windows. Things out of place unnerved him, and he went and yanked the paper off, and scanned it briefly.

It should have made him relax, it should have allowed him to register, *no threat, stand down.*

No phone, it read, *Did you still want me and Tuck to come for supper at your place tomorrow? Love, Serenity.*

Love. As if Serenity had a clue what that was.

Of course, neither did he.

Instead of standing down, he felt he was on red alert. Wordlessly he handed Grace the note, and saw the little smile tickle her lips when she read Tucker's name.

"You invited them over to your place? For supper?" He folded his arms over his chest and glared at her. Melbourne seemed to be fading by the second.

"Yes." She looked defiant, having correctly read by his tone he did not approve of Serenity and Tucker being invited to her house.

"I don't think you should."

The last of the dazed look left her face. "Don't think that just because you gave me a perfect day and an okay kiss, you can boss me around."

An okay kiss? "You didn't have to invite them to your house, for God's sake. If you're worried about the kid being hungry, you could have taken them for a pizza."

Shoot. He had not played that one very well. He could tell by the stricken look that crossed her face it had not occurred to her that Tucker might be hungry.

That's what you got when you grew up in a perfect world. Despite what she wanted to believe, Grace had been sheltered. A home where there wasn't enough food on the table had never crossed her mind. And never would have if he hadn't opened his big mouth.

The stricken look was quickly replaced with one of pure stubbornness.

"I'll invite whomever I please for dinner. And what's more, Rory Adams, I am not looking for anyone to run my life. I would only be interested in a relationship of equals."

"A what?" he sputtered.

"Never mind."

"A relationship?" he said, incredulous.

"I didn't mean it the way you are taking it."

"You're blushing."

"I'm sunburned."

"You should know I am not a guy who is interested in a relationship of any kind. Not equals. Not unequals."

For a moment she scanned his face, and he steeled himself, daring her to see the yearning that had nearly swallowed him earlier.

"I'm not looking for a relationship, either!" she protested.

"You just said—

"That just slipped out. I meant it generically, as in no kind of woman with any sense of her self would tolerate being bossed around."

"Directed," he inserted.

"Whatever! Personally, I'm not looking for a relationship of any kind. I'm done with that sort of thing. I'm a career woman. And a very successful one."

"That's not true, Grace."

Her jaw dropped. "It is. I can show you my financial statements!"

"I wasn't referring to your success at business. I don't believe you're done with that sort of thing, the big wedding followed by the cute house followed by a baby. And then another one. Three. I bet you want three."

"I don't. I'm done with those dreams!"

"I can see in your face that you're not. I can see in your face exactly what you're looking for. What you'll always look for—what your mom and dad had. A perfect family to go with your perfect days. The cottage in the summer. The Thanksgiving turkey. The big Christmas hoopla."

"After the breakup of my relationship I've decided none of that is for me."

"I can clearly see what is making you such easy prey for Serenity."

"I am not her prey! What an ugly thing to say!"

Ugly. Raw. Cynical. That's what he was. It made him unworthy of her kisses, but maybe it also made him the perfect one to deflect Serenity.

"You think you've given up on your hopes and dreams, but you really haven't."

"I have!"

"They've just gone underground. Serenity knows what you want. You'd give your right arm for Tucker to be Graham's. A substitute for that baby you thought you and Henry were going to have."

"Stop it!"

He could see angry little spots of color on both her cheeks. Good. He had succeeded at nipping any attraction she was feeling for him in the bud. So he shrugged. "Okay."

Just as suddenly as it had come, her anger was gone. "Don't you want Tucker to be Graham's son?"

The truth was it was much easier to contemplate Tucker *not* being Graham's, and that's how he was playing it until he had cold, hard proof that showed him differently.

"I'm coming for dinner tomorrow," he announced.

"You're not! I haven't invited you."

"I'm not letting you deal with Serenity on your own. You're naive. You're way too innocent."

"I am not innocent," she sputtered. "What on earth would give you that idea?"

The fact you could barely wear that bathing suit. Your kiss.

"Let me help you deal with it," he said quietly.

For a moment she looked stubborn. But then she looked at the note in her hand and he saw the doubt on her face.

"I won't say anything to Serenity," he said, playing that doubt. "I'll let you handle it. But I'll be there, gauging what she says, running it through the meter of my cynicism. I'll offer you my opinion after, but I won't force it on you."

And if I pocket a spoon with a little saliva sample on it, who's that hurting?

"All right," she said, clearly unhappy with the surrender, unhappy that she was accepting what she needed most and wanted least.

Not to do this alone.

"Where do you live?" he asked.

"I bought the house from my parents when they moved, so I live where I always lived," she said with stiff pride, as if the fact she had never left her family home proved everything he had just said about her.

And it did, didn't it?

He sighed. "What time should I be there?"

"Fiveish?"

In the world he had started moving in, dinner didn't happen at five. It happened at eight or nine. After cocktails. And hors d'oeuvres. After endless small talk, and sometimes a little careless flirting with people who were no more interested in relationships than he was.

The banality of it all suddenly made him feel like his world had become unbearably lonely.

He was being pulled into her little world. And he didn't like it. But he was just going to have to suck it up until this Serenity situation was cleared up.

And then nothing, but nothing—not even the memory of the way Grace's lips had tasted crushed beneath his own—was going to keep him from personally supervising that job in Australia.

CHAPTER SIX

"Mr. Adams, are you all right?"

"Huh?" Rory had been staring aimlessly out his office window. He'd had the dream last night. Worse than normal. The two teenage boys, the bullets. This time, he had ducked, as if he could see the bullet coming, as if he had deliberately let Graham get it instead of him.

And still, there was a sense of having awoken too soon. There was still a piece missing, something important. Words.

Not that it mattered. There were no words that could make him feel better, that could take away this feeling of tremendous guilt. There were no words that could make the realization of a man's powerlessness over life and death any easier.

Sometimes, you couldn't protect the people you cared about. His mother. Graham. Was the dream more intense because he had spent time with Gracie? Because he was seeing how his inability to stop bad things from happening had gone out like a wave and swamped other lives?

If he could protect Grace from Serenity would it make up for all his past failings?

"I'm fine," he said gruffly to Bridey. "I've been invited out for dinner tonight. Could you get me something to bring?"

"The regular?"

"Yeah, whatever." What was the regular? A bottle of good wine, exquisitely expensive, roses in the same price range. "No, wait."

He didn't want to bring wine if Serenity was there. She'd probably swig it all back and then try to drive herself and the kid somewhere.

And he actually didn't want wine with Grace again, either. Because after one glass at lunch, she'd lost her inhibitions enough to put on a bikini.

And kiss him.

A kiss powerful enough to send a man packing to Australia!

"Uh, no wine," he said. "And not roses for the flowers, either." Somehow, Grace wasn't a rose kind of girl in his mind. "Something less, uh, formal. Less, uh, ostentatious."

"Got it," Bridey said.

He arrived at Grace's feeling foolishly like a boy on his first date. He wished he hadn't brought the flowers at all, because the bouquet was quite large, a colorful explosion of daisies and daffodils, mums and lilies.

There was no sign of Serenity's decrepit old truck yet.

He looked at the house—Graham's house, really—and waited for the sadness of the memories of them together here to hit. They didn't and he felt thankful for all that Grace had done to it. She had made the house her own, painted, changed the facade, added colorful plantings beneath the windows and up the walkway.

She came to the door, and he found himself steeling himself—not against memories of him and Graham, but against memories of him and her.

And the way her lips had tasted: the hint of passion in them, the faint eagerness. And the way she had made him feel.

As if he could trust her. As if he could trust her with things he had told no one.

She opened the door and looked over his shoulder. "No Ferrari today," she said. "Hello, Rory."

"I traded it in on something a little more me."

"The Ferrari was you." She studied the 1965 Chev truck parked at the curb, and said, "That's you, too. Ah, a man of many faces."

She meant it lightly, but he didn't take it that way. He *was* a man of many faces, and some of them would probably terrify her. That would be a good thing for her to remember. That he was not always what he seemed.

She took the flowers with such genuine delight that he was glad he'd brought them after all.

"Daffodils in July!" she said. "Imagine that! Come in."

The house, too, was completely changed and he felt some stress he had been holding leave him.

"You've fixed this up," he said.

"I love my house. I'm afraid my idea of a good time is hanging out at the hardware store mooning over engineered flooring and cabinet pulls."

So, it was exactly as he had guessed. She wanted to pass herself off as a career woman, but she was pretty solidly invested in the whole concept of home.

And she had it so right. The living room he was looking at was a relaxed space, but everything from the furniture choices to the paint colors invited you to feel at home, to relax, to sit and maybe to stay for a long, long time. There was even a teddy bear nestled among the couch cushions that didn't look the least ridiculous. It added to the cozy feeling of just coming home.

There was a feeling here of safety.

He frowned at that. He felt safe. Why wouldn't he feel safe? He wasn't in the land of blood and sand and tears anymore. And he was never going back there.

Though, standing in her living room, he was acutely aware maybe he had not totally ever left that land.

Because a place like this—cozy, inviting—was foreign to him. The whole concept of home was foreign to him. His own houses growing up had always been temporary. Sooner than later, his family would be moving all their broken furniture and chipped dishes. No nice touches like those yellow-shaded lamps or the Finnish rug on the floor.

And his place now?

A showpiece of modern design. All black leather, steel, shiny surfaces, hard angles. It had a temporary feel to it. And it *was* temporary. He bought real estate as an investment. He did not attach to it.

He had not known he wanted "homey" until he saw this.

"Come through to the kitchen," she said. "I'm peeling spuds. I thought Tucker might like homemade fries. I hope you don't mind. The menu is pretty kid-friendly tonight. Burgers. Fries. Milkshakes."

"Mind? That's a menu out of every man's dream."

That earned a smile, and then she led him to the

kitchen, which also reflected more changes to the foot-print of the old house. A wall had been dispensed with, the kitchen, dining room and living room were all seam-less, one harmonious space.

She set him down on a stool at a granite countertop island that gave a hint of separation between the kitchen and the other spaces.

He picked up a knife and tackled a heap of potatoes while she ripped lettuce into bite-size portions for a salad.

He was aware of feeling at home here. Not just the setting. But with her.

He pursued that sense of safety. Music was play-ing softly in the background. A cat wound around the leg of his chair. Everything was in order, but not in an uptight way. This was a space where a person could relax. Where there would rarely be a raised voice. Or the sound of dishes breaking in anger. And maybe that, alone, made it one of the most dangerous places he had ever been.

Rory Adams was in her space. He put down the knife after cutting the potatoes into fries. He was looking as at home here as if he had been born to this space.

She glanced at the clock.

"They're late," she said.

"The thing about a girl like Serenity?"

Grace truly hated it that he was such a self-proclaimed expert on girls like Serenity, but she man-aged to bite her tongue. "Yes?"

"They're always late."

"How do you know so much about girls like

Serenity?" She tried for a teasing note, but was pretty sure she failed. She was scared about his answer, but when he was silent for a long, long time, she wasn't sure he would answer.

"She's like my mother."

And she remembered him again, out on the street that night long ago, taking his mother's elbow.

He was concentrating fiercely on the potato, as if what he had just said didn't matter.

But she knew it did. She knew it mattered that he told her things like that.

"Tell me how you and Graham came to know Serenity."

"*Know* is stretching it a touch," he said. "We had ten days leave before we were shipping out. I think it was that first time, Afghanistan. We were shipping out from Edmonton, and the Calgary Stampede was on. None of us had ever been to it, so we decided to go. Calgary is only a couple of hours drive from Edmonton.

"Guys being guys, we had to make a few pit stops along the way. Quite a few, actually. Finally, we stopped in this rinky-dink little town not far from Calgary, and they were having their own little second-rate Stampede and rodeo.

"Serenity was running her ponies as part of the midway, plus riding a horse in the barrel-racing competition. Somehow, we got partying with all those rodeo and fairground people, and we never quite made the Calgary Stampede. And never had any regrets about it, either."

She read his face. "Until now."

"You know, when you're shipping out and facing the very real possibility you might not be coming back, life has this intensity to it. It's a kind of a high. But it does not involve consequences. Not one of us—including Graham—ever glanced back at those few crazy days before we left."

"So, there is a very real possibility that Tucker is Graham's?"

"Well, it's one possibility. But it doesn't add up, Grace. Why would she wait until now to let you know?"

"I'm going to ask her, point-blank, tonight if Tucker is Graham's. And if he is, why she didn't let Graham know that."

"I think that's a good plan."

She recognized it as a weakness that she liked having his approval. But like many good plans it had a flaw: it relied on Serenity showing up, and by six, Grace was beginning to acknowledge maybe she wasn't going to. And also acknowledging how eagerly she had wanted to see Tucker again, searching his face and his mannerisms for traces of Graham.

And the part she hadn't admitted to Rory? That she was finding more evidence all the time. The crooked way he smiled, the way his hair grew in a little swirl at the crown of his head, the stubborn set of his mouth, the way he walked.

"Are you starving?" she asked.

"I don't mind waiting."

But by six-thirty, she knew they had waited long enough. "I'll cook some for us, and leave some, just in case..."

Cooking with him almost took away the pang that Tucker and Serenity had not arrived.

It was fun having a man who knew what he was

doing at the grill. It was a cozy little scene: one she had imagined a million times when she was laboring over this little space.

Imagined it with Harold. Cozy evenings of cooking together, an easy companionship, a sense of home that she had never one-hundred-percent achieved by herself, much as she had tried.

And now this. Rory Adams in her kitchen, peeling potatoes, taking charge of the hamburgers, laughing at her concern that the flames were leaping too high in the grill. The problem with having a man like this in your space?

Would it ever feel totally like your space again, or would it always seem slightly lacking, no matter what you did?

There was no way a cat, a career and a penchant for decorating magazines was ever going to make her feel like this: zingy with an electrical energy, suffused with laughter, *so aware.* Certainly she had seen a man standing at a grill before, but had she ever noticed the small details of that experience? The smell in the air, the way he did little things with such a supreme confidence in himself?

She had imagined an evening like this with Harold, and they had even had evenings similar to this. So why had it never felt like this? Always a faint discontent between them, something that stifled instead of invigorated.

For the first time since her engagement had ended, Grace could truly see it as a blessing, and not just pay lip service to the whole concept of "if it was meant to be, it would be."

It was seven-fifteen by the time they had finished eating and cleaning up. He had cheerfully buried himself up to his elbows in suds, cleaning her difficult grill, flicking soap with playful threat in her direction when she tried to help.

Without warning, the elation left her. It felt as if it hissed out of her like air out of a punctured balloon. And in its place was disappointment.

It was disappointment that Tucker and Serenity had failed to show up.

Disappointment that this was not really her life. Rory Adams wasn't here because he wanted to be with her. Because he'd found her kiss impossible to back away from. No, he was here to protect her.

And the thing he thought she needed protecting from wasn't coming. The dishes were done. They had eaten. There was absolutely no reason for him to stay here— or for her to want him to.

"Well," she said, trying to inject a note of cheer into her voice, "I guess they aren't coming. I took out my favorite board game for nothing."

"You have a favorite board game?"

"I do. And everyone should. Tucker looks like he's never played a board game in his life. Can you imagine?"

"Actually, I can."

"You've never played a board game?" She was incredulous. At first she thought he must be pulling her leg. Then she read in his face, that he was not.

Girlfriend, she told herself sternly, *send him home. Something is happening here. You are getting in way too deep.*

But a person who had never played board games? It was practically like saying you had never had a childhood.

She thought of his house, that night he had walked out to rescue his mother. Not very old then, already a man.

Rory Adams was the man least likely to need rescuing. He was all easy confidence and male grace. He was all sensual appeal. No doubt women had been throwing themselves at him since he had learned to blink.

She had not been a blip on his radar eight years ago, and she was only a little more than that now. He was the CEO of a big company. He could conjure cowboys and cars out of thin air.

What about that would make her think he would enjoy a silly board game?

"Would you like to try it?" She tried for careless aplomb, she sounded shy and faintly strangled.

Was she desperately holding on to this, her perfect evening? A matched set. Her perfect day yesterday, her perfect evening tonight.

The thing about having achieved perfection? Did you ever want to go back to just normal again? Ordinary? Could you? Or did you crave it now? A person who had slept in silk sheets did not want to go back to burlap sacking after all!

He studied her, and she had the horrible feeling he knew what it had cost her to ask him, that a frightened fourteen-year-old waited for rejection, a sneering laugh.

"Sure, I'll play with you. Don't give up yet, in Serenity's world, fashionably late could mean midnight."

Suddenly playing a silly game, intended for children, seemed ridiculous. He'd told her about his company. He wasn't playing for entertainment. He was rubbing shoulders with race-car drivers and the jet set. He probably couldn't wait to get out of here, was being held here by some sense of obligation.

"You don't have to stay, you can go."

"Nah. I'll stay."

"Because you don't want me to deal with Serenity by myself if she does turn up?"

"Well, if she turns up at this time of night, you might want someone around who can wrestle her truck keys from her."

"That poor kid. Poor Tucker."

"That's why I'll stay. Because you seem sad. It's no fun being sad by yourself."

"No, really."

"No, really. Haul out the game."

Don't, she told herself. But she did.

"I think you can play with two," she said, getting her game off the sideboard, and putting it on the kitchen island. The box was faded with age, and all the corners were held together with tape that had turned dark yellow. "But it's more fun with four."

"We'll be two people each then. I'll be Nasty Ned and Roaring Rory and you be Goodie Two Shoes Grace and Sideswipe Sally."

"I am not going to be Goodie Two Shoes!"

"Okay. You pick who you're going to be." He had already retrieved the instructions and, after a quick skim, began setting up pieces.

"I'll be Racy Gracie!"

"Good one. No stealing kisses from me, though."

"That wasn't really a kiss," she said, flustered.

"It wasn't? You could have fooled me. And I would have thought I kind of knew a kiss when one was planted on my lips, but if you say it wasn't…"

She could feel the heat move up her face. "It was just a thank you, for such a nice day."

"Uh-huh. You be careful about thanking all the boys that way, or you really will be Racy Gracie."

"Oh!"

"What are we playing for, by the way?"

"You don't play a game like this *for* anything. You just play it for fun."

And this was fun for her, damn him. The light teasing, the familiarity, his willingness to do something dumb.

"For fun?" He snorted. "Soldiers don't play anything for fun. They'll bet a week's wages on which spider is going to cross the room first. There has to be something at stake."

"What would you like to play for?"

"How about that teddy bear on the couch?"

"I got that out for Tucker. I don't still have a teddy bear."

"Gracie, that kid is not a teddy-bear kind of kid. Or a board-game kind of kid, either."

"Well, you didn't strike me as either of those things, either, but here we are, playing a board game for my teddy bear."

"I knew it was yours," he said triumphantly.

"Well, maybe you're not quite the tough guy you seem, either, since you want to take him home."

"It's not really about the teddy bear. He must mean something to you. So it would be fun to take it away."

"That's awful!"

"I know," he said happily.

"So, what's at stake for you? What am I going to take from you when I win?"

He eyed her lips for a moment. "You choose."

She eyed his lips for a moment. No, too dangerous. Akin to playing strip poker. Over a board game. That would be degenerate!

She snapped her fingers. "The CD we listened to going up the lake."

"Ouch."

"Perfect," she purred happily.

"This has become a high-stakes game, Miss Day."

"My favorite kind," she said, and then they were both laughing at the absurdity of her ever having played high-stakes anything.

She won three games in a row. With great grumbling he went and retrieved his CD. It was now closing in on nine.

Time to send him home. Because something was happening to her heart. She was realizing she could fall for this man so fast and so hard it would make anything she had ever experienced before seem as lackluster as porridge congealing in a pot.

"Can I listen to it one more time before I surrender it?" he asked.

He couldn't possibly think Serenity was still going to show, but part of her was so hungry for more time with him that she didn't care, she threw caution to the wind.

She knew, after all, she had to walk away from this.

For her own self-preservation. Only yesterday he had told her in no uncertain terms what he thought of relationships.

And she had agreed with him. But she might have been lying. Even to herself. So, after tonight, she would keep her distance. She would.

But she felt like someone who loved chocolate being told they could never have it again. Except for one last taste.

Who could resist that?

And so Grace made them milkshakes and they sat on the sofa, side by side, listening to the CD.

He was so relaxed, sprawled out on her sofa. She had not been aware of some finely held tension that was intrinsic to him until now that it was gone.

It seemed to her the whole evening had been so filled with simple things, and yet it had felt suffused with light.

She wanted to kiss him again.

She was pretty sure he wanted to kiss her, too.

She leaned toward him, and the tension was back in him.

"Don't, Gracie. There's things you need to know. About me."

But she didn't want to know those things if they would stop her from wanting to kiss him, and she had the sense that that was why he wanted to tell her. She wanted the barriers ripped down, he wanted them up.

"I need to tell you about Graham. When I'm done you'll know who I really am."

Unspoken, she heard, *And you won't like it.*

Strangely, when Rory had first contacted her, Grace had heard this very moment coming.

She had thought she was not ready to hear what he had to say. She had thought she would never be ready. That was why she had said, *I can't see why we need to talk.*

But suddenly she could see exactly why they needed to talk. Suddenly, she was ready.

Somewhere, somehow, she had become less interested in protecting herself. Somehow, more was being required of her. She needed to hear what he had to say. To save them both.

Rory was silent for a long time. Finally, working past the lump in his throat, he managed to say, "I was with him when he died."

When he had contacted her when he got home, this is precisely the conversation he had been determined to have. He wanted her to know he'd been with her brother when he died. That he had not been alone. That he had not been afraid. That Graham's last thought had been of her.

Why was it so hard to do it, then?

Because he wasn't expecting that moment—fear and chaos and ultimately death—to be superimposed over this one—laughter, safety, feeling relaxed.

Happy again.

And because all that—that Graham had not been alone or afraid—was only part of the truth. The real truth was his failure, and she needed to know that before they traded kisses.

She needed to know it all before she offered him her lips.

"I'm ready," she said, and he saw the bravery in her and saw that she was ready.

He closed his eyes. He could feel the heat and smell the dust. And other smells. Garbage. Sewage. Death.

"It was a pretty ordinary day for over there. Too hot. We were on patrol. It was average. You're always alert, scanning, but none of the signs were there.

"Then I saw these two teenage boys. I felt like something was wrong, but I didn't react right away. I'm not sure why. Maybe because it was so hot. Maybe because they just seemed so young. Maybe because they hadn't done anything. It's not as if they were reaching under their robes to pull out submachine guns.

"But I knew something was off, and I didn't react fast enough. One of them glanced up, touched his nose. I guess it was a signal. And the next thing I knew there were bullets flying everywhere.

"I ducked behind a wall. And I looked for Graham and was shocked that he wasn't right with me. He was always right with me. We always had each other's backs. Always. He was out there in the street. He'd already been hit.

"I went and got him, dragged him back to cover. He was alive, but it was already too late."

He frowned. Just like in the dream, he knew there was a part of this missing, a part his mind refused to remember. Important words.

But what could be more important to Grace than the fact she had been one of the last things on her brother's mind?

"I just wanted you to know that he wasn't alone. That I was there. And I wanted you to know that he wasn't afraid. I wanted you to know his last thoughts were of you. He wanted you to be okay."

He glanced at her. She was crying.

"I'm so sorry, Grace."

"No. I'm so glad you told me. I needed to know, even though I was scared to find out. I needed to know that he wasn't alone. I needed to know he wasn't afraid. And I know it will bring me great comfort that his last thoughts were of me."

She wasn't getting it. He obviously had not been plain enough. She seemed to be looking at him with a graver sense of connection instead of less of one.

"Grace, I didn't have his back. I failed him."

It couldn't be more plain than that.

The tears came harder. "Oh, Rory," she whispered. "Don't do that to yourself. Please."

Now, she was right over beside him, her arms were around him, her warm tears were spilling down his chest.

"No," she said. "I will not allow you to carry that burden one step further. It was not your fault."

"I saw the boys."

"And what should you have done when you saw them? What should you have done differently?"

"I don't know," he said, and it was a terrible admission, that he did not know how he could have changed things. Even now, looking back, even visiting it every night in his dreams, he did not know. He suspected he could have done something.

And that he had failed to do it.

And that was the part that was missing from his dream and from his memory.

And he hated that feeling more than any other.

And himself, for not knowing.

"I should have pushed Graham out of the way. I should have been the one who took it. Jesus, Gracie, why not me, instead of him? Your whole family torn apart. I don't have a family to be torn apart."

This was going all wrong. All wrong.

He had planned for this to be his secret weapon. His way to stop the growing attraction between them.

He was the man responsible for her brother's death. That should make her pull away and fast.

But the effect seemed to be the exact opposite.

She was doing what he had never been able to do. She was forgiving him. She was accepting that he was just a man who had not been able to stop the unfolding of destiny.

She was scanning his face.

"You're not really doing okay, are you?"

Why was it that she could see that? Everyone else, even his brother, thought he was the successful businessman. They didn't know he was running.

And he didn't want her to know, either. He didn't want to burden her.

And yet, he could not stop himself, he could not hold the words back.

"I have dreams. In every single dream I am responsible."

"How often do you have those dreams?" Her voice was so soft, and the tenderness in her eyes was making him *want* to tell her. Why? What earthly good could come from sharing this terrible burden with her?

"I have them every night," he said. "Sometimes half a dozen times a night."

"So, what are they telling you that you won't admit during the day?" she asked.

He closed his eyes. He recognized the million-dollar question when he heard it. He made one last desperate effort to make her understand.

"I know it's my fault," he said, his voice hoarse. "We looked out for each other. I let him down. I let him die."

He waited for her to say something patronizing that he could hate her for, that would allow him to rebuild this wall that had tumbled down. He waited for her to say something about survivor's guilt and it wasn't his fault at all.

She didn't say anything. He dared to look at her, and saw the tears still sliding down her face.

Only now, they were not for her brother.

They were for him.

It felt as if she was reaching inside him and taking the pain. Sharing it. Understanding it. It wasn't pity.

It was compassion so pure that it stole his breath and what was left of his strength.

He reached for her, took her wrists, marveled at their delicacy and pulled her into his chest. She came to him easily, and he rested his chin on the top of her head, and felt her surrender, melting into him like warm putty.

He breathed in her scent and held her.

"Do you think we'll ever be okay again?" she asked after a long, long time.

"Right now I am," he said, and was surprised how much he meant it. "Right now I am."

She thought about it, changed her position so she could tilt her head up and look at him. "Me, too," she decided.

And then she pulled away from him, and scanned his face, saw something there that reassured her and she tucked herself back into him.

And it just was.

Her breath rising with his breath.

Her heart beating with his heart.

Her warmth melting into his warmth.

Her softness feeling so good against all in him that was unyielding.

Rory had just told Grace the worst thing about himself. He knew he'd been saving that confession as his out, as his way of driving her away if things got too complicated between them.

He could not have predicted that the exact opposite would happen. She seemed to trust him more, not less.

And he did not feel deserving of that.

The courageous thing to do would be to tell her good-bye.

But he didn't feel courageous. This house, and Gracie, had been chipping away at his armor.

And he felt, without his really being aware, he had been stripped of it completely.

He wanted to hold her, just like this, for as long as he could make this moment last.

But he of all people should know that moments like this one, filled with unearthly quiet, moments of nothing that held everything, were way too rare.

And always brief.

And the calm before the storm was called that for a reason. There was always a storm.

And it came.

They heard the truck coming from a long way off, the boom-boom of the untuned diesel engine, the shriek of a corner taken too fast.

They were both up and at her window when Serenity's very distinctive truck veered in behind his own, jumped the curb and came to rest in the very center of Grace's front lawn.

CHAPTER SEVEN

"I<small>F</small> she's driving like that with the kid in there with her—" Rory didn't finish the sentence, and he didn't have to. He bolted for the front door and went out, bypassing her front staircase in a single leap. Grace was hard on his heels.

He arrived on the passenger side of the truck, its engine off but the headlights eerily illuminating the yard while making it impossible to see the vehicle's interior.

Rory yanked open the passenger door. Serenity must have been leaning hard against it, because she didn't so much fall as spill out. Despite his surprise, Rory dived and managed to catch her before she hit the ground.

He straightened, staring down at the woman in his arms, shocked to find her there, more shocked by her slightness. Holding Serenity was like holding a wounded sparrow.

Her body was completely limp, and there was no warmth to it. She was unnaturally pale. When he bent and put his nose close to her slightly parted lips there was no smell of alcohol, but she was barely breathing.

He glanced up. "What the hell?"

It was Tucker, wide-eyed with fear, behind the wheel of the truck. Astonished, Rory saw the boy had used duct tape to fasten blocks of wood to the brake, gas and clutch pedals. Ingenious? Or not the first time he had driven the huge vehicle?

"My mama's so sick," Tucker said, his voice choked with fear. "I didn't know what to do. We don't have a phone."

"You did exactly the right thing," Rory said. "Come on. Get out of the truck. Grace, start your car. We're going to the hospital."

"Mama said no," Tucker said plaintively. "We ain't got no money. We don't have no medical insurance."

"I'll look after it," Rory said, adjusting the slight weight he carried, moving toward where Grace had her vehicle going. He glanced over his shoulder.

The boy looked at him suspiciously, and then he drew in a deep breath, and his face crumpled. He hid his face in his shirtsleeve.

Rory knew by pure instinct that he could not acknowledge those tears from a boy who had probably spent his whole life trying to be tough and hard and strong.

"Go get in Grace's car, now. Your mama's going to be okay," Rory said. Of course, he had no idea if that was true, but he knew he had to be both calm and firm.

He was a man who could claim a lot of experience dealing with men who were young and who were frightened. Maybe not this young and maybe not this frightened, but it was all the same thing.

He could not show a flicker of doubt, even if, feeling Serenity's limp form in his arms as he went to Grace's car and got in the backseat, that's exactly what he felt.

Grace was already in the driver's seat, and she

glanced back at him, and he saw something in her face. That she was counting on him, too, to somehow make this all right. The truth? He did not want to be counted on to be anyone's hero.

And yet, at the very same time, a man could come to live for the look on Gracie's face.

All night, Grace had felt herself falling.

Falling for Rory Adams.

All over again. Just as she had been foolish enough to do at fourteen.

The sensation of falling had only increased when he had told her about her brother, when she had sensed the enormous burden he had shouldered by himself for way, way too long.

Now that sensation increased again as Grace watched Rory in the emergency room of the hospital. It was obvious he had become an expert on crisis. His demeanor was one of complete calm.

The emergency room unnerved her. She could hear a child wailing, a man in a chair in the waiting room had blood seeping through the white dressing that was wrapped around his head. A mother paced and made reassuring noises to the quiet baby in her arms. A woman slept in one of the chairs, oblivious to the drama around her.

But Rory, his hands full of Serenity, was not distracted. He paused only for a moment in the doorway, scanning, and he seemed to know by pure instinct where to go and who was in charge. He found a nurse, followed her through swinging doors that said No Admittance. Tucker followed.

That left Grace to deal with the thorny issue of admittance. Beyond Serenity's name Grace knew little about her.

But after a while Rory was back at her side, Tucker stuck to him like an orphaned pup looking for a pack leader.

Between him and Tucker they were able to provide the admitting clerk with Serenity's birth date and some other basic information.

When the question of health insurance came up, Rory didn't even hesitate. He guaranteed payment and backed it up with a credit card that made the admitting clerk raise her eyebrows.

Finally, he led Tucker to one of those hard plastic chairs, sat him down, went to a vending machine and got him a soda and some potato chips.

Grace and Rory both watched as the boy wolfed down the food.

"When do you think he ate last?" Grace asked.

"Don't ask," Rory said, nudging her. They moved away from him a bit.

"They're going to have to admit Serenity," he said. "What are we going to do about him?"

We.

Even in this chaotic, somewhat frightening situation, she allowed herself to savor that.

We. As if they were a team. And if she were on a team? Wouldn't she pick his? He was a leader. He could be counted on to make hard decisions in difficult circumstances.

He was the kind of man everyone wanted on their side when the chips were down. If you were in a hotel that was on fire and saw him coming through the smoke, you would know you were going to be okay. If you were on a ship that was going down in rough seas, he was the one you would follow to the life raft.

And he knew he was that kind of man, so no wonder he felt so acutely responsible for Graham's death.

And so it was time for her not to let him take the lead, not to accept him taking full responsibility. She had to be worthy of him.

And that meant she had to be as strong as he was, as responsible for the decision-making process.

"What do you mean what are we going to do about him?" she asked.

"I think we should call the authorities," he said in a low tone.

"The authorities? No." She said it firmly, his equal.

Something in her tone made Tucker look up from licking salt and chip crumbs off his fingers. He regarded them both with deep wariness.

"Shh. If he catches wind that we're going to turn him over, he'll run like a rabbit."

"Well, we aren't turning him over," she said, stubbornly. The problem with these alpha types? They always thought they knew what was right. They relied only on themselves.

It was too lonely. She was not going to let Rory be that lonely anymore.

"Look, you can't just take somebody's kid because you want to. It's not like we're his family."

"We don't know that yet. I might be his aunt."

"That's a big *might*."

"Let's just ask him if he has anyone we can call for him," she asked, hearing the leadership in her voice.

Rory looked doubtful. "If he had anyone to call I don't think he would have driven a truck that he couldn't even reach the pedals on to your place in the middle of the night and parked in the middle of your lawn."

"I am not sending him with strangers."

"Grace, *we're* practically strangers to him."

A nurse came out and beckoned to Rory. She was young and extraordinarily beautiful, despite a certain no-nonsense look about her. Grace could not help but notice the respect shown to Rory. It was as if people who dealt in crisis recognized each other, belonged to a secret club.

The nurse put her hand on Rory's arm.

Grace felt a little shiver of shocking jealousy, though the gesture was no more than casual contact.

Still, she felt herself bracing for his reaction. Despite the situation, would he wink? Smile that disarming smile? Touch her back ever so lightly?

But Rory did not reciprocate in any way. If he had noticed the beauty of the nurse it did not show. In fact, with a slightly curt nod, he slid his arm out from under the nurse's touch and came to Grace.

"They are admitting Serenity," he said in an undertone. "They have no idea what's wrong. She's in and out of consciousness, not well enough to give them any clues."

"I'll tell him," Grace said, and went to Tucker. She squatted on her heels, not wanting to intimidate him by looking down at him.

"Hey, buddy," Grace said quietly. She saw he didn't like her calling him buddy.

In her peripheral vision she was aware of Rory standing close, waiting to take it if she needed him to, but letting her have the lead.

She was not quite sure what she had done to earn Tucker's animosity, but it made her aware they were strangers, that maybe Rory was right. There were people trained to deal with these situations.

But this child, this frightened, hungry, brave little boy might be Graham's. She might be his aunt. She could not abandon him. She could not. He, a little boy, had driven a truck, that he had no business driving, to her house. Trusting her, overcoming his mystifying dislike, believing she would do the right thing by him and his mother.

"They're going to keep your mom here for a while," she said.

"Is she okay?"

"She's in very good hands. They'll look after her."

Tucker looked at her, searching her face for truth. She could tell he was trying very hard not to cry, "What do you want to do, Tucker?"

He looked suddenly frail and exhausted. "I gotta look after the ponies. They never got fed tonight."

The answer nearly broke her heart. So small, so much weight on his shoulders.

"I'll look after them," Rory said. "I think you should go with Grace. She's got a spare room. You can stay with her tonight and we'll see how your mom is doing in the morning."

"You don't know nothing about looking after ponies," Tucker said, managing a note of scornful pride despite his fear and exhaustion. "And I'm coming back here after, to be with my mama."

"How about Slim McKenzie?" Rory said, down on his heels now, too, not missing a beat. "Would you trust him to look after your ponies?"

Something shifted in Tucker's face at the mention of Slim.

"Yeah, Slim could do it. And then I could stay here with my mom."

"Here's the thing, Tucker," Rory said, his voice tempered with the most exquisite patience, "I don't think they're going to let you stay with your mom. But I'll give you my cell phone, and I'll tell that nurse over there you're going to be checking in, all night long if you want to. Is that okay?"

"I don't want to stay with her," Tucker said, jerking his chin at Grace.

Again, Grace wondered what she had done to deserve his animosity, tried not to take it personally.

"If you don't want to stay with me, I'm sure you can stay with Rory," she said soothingly.

Rory glared at her, came off his heels and took her elbow. He took her off a bit from where Tucker was watching them. "No. That's just weird. Men do not take little boys they don't know home with them."

"I'll come, too, then." She could feel it again. Doing this with him. Not leaving him to the loneliness of making every decision by himself, being so responsible. "Do you have two spare rooms?"

"Unfortunately. Why do I have the feeling you're

going to get us all arrested? Or leave us wide open to being blackmailed by Serenity?"

"I think she'll be nothing but appreciative."

He snorted, but if she was not mistaken, he was taking to the novelty of having someone share the decision-making process with him.

"Unless you have a better idea?"

But he didn't. Still glaring at her, he fished his cell phone out of his pocket. "Slim. Sorry. I know it's late. I have a bit of an emergency I need your help with." He outlined it, listened to Slim's calm reply. "Thanks. Okay. Ponies looked after. Let's go."

And that's how Grace found herself at Rory Adams's super-posh bachelor pad in a condo on the shores of Lake Okanagan.

"Wow," Tucker said from the backseat when they drove up to the building. "You're rich."

"Don't tell your mother," Rory muttered under his breath, and Grace gave him a little kick.

They got out of her car, and she tried not to be too overawed by the building. She dealt with wealthy people all the time. But still, this was probably the most sought-after address in the entire Okanagan Valley.

The Monashee was an exclusive building engineered right into a cliff that overlooked the night-blackened and restless waters of the lake. They pulled up at the front entrance; the building looked like ten stories of nothing but glass.

"Holy…" Tucker said, getting out of the car and staring up at the architecture. The *holy* was then followed by a word that shocked Grace, not because she had never heard the word before, but because she had never heard it come from a seven-year-old boy!

"You don't say that word in front of a lady," Rory said, but without heat, without that kind of frightening firmness he had shown those teenage boys on the float. It was obvious Tucker was beyond exhaustion, and Grace appreciated Rory for knowing intuitively how to deal with him.

A valet came and took her car, and Rory ushered them through a lobby that reminded Grace of a very expensive hotel. Deep leather couches sat on handwoven Armenian carpets on highly polished marble floors. A black granite wall had water sliding silently down it.

They got on an elevator that opened directly into Rory's apartment.

It was an open space, but as different from hers as a camel was different from a kangaroo. Everything was muted opulence: white sleek furniture, Brazilian-cherry flooring, art that was obviously not from the poster bin at the discount store. The entire back wall was a sheet of glass that overlooked the lake.

"Holy..." Tucker said again, but this time, with a glance at Rory, excluded the second word.

"Do you want something to eat?" Rory asked.

The little boy contemplated this, but then shook his head. Rory showed them through to a guest wing: two beautiful bedrooms that shared one extraordinarily glamorous bathroom.

Within minutes, without even taking off his clothes, Rory's cell phone in his hand with the hospital on speed dial, Tucker was fast asleep in between pure-silk sheets.

Unwrapping a toothbrush in the guest bathroom to brush his teeth seemed to be all he could manage.

Grace gazed at him tenderly for a moment. He looked so small in the huge bed. She resisted the impulse to brush his hair back from his pale forehead and plant a kiss there, and backed out of the room with a whispered good-night.

She recognized her own exhaustion and how vulnerable it made her. When she came out of Tucker's room and saw Rory silhouetted at his floor-to-ceiling living-room window, she wanted to go to him.

To cast the last of her caution to the wind.

But he sensed she was there and turned to her.

She wanted to say, *Come hold me, let's go back to that moment before that truck ended up parked in my front yard.*

Instead she said, "Poor kid was done. He could barely brush his teeth."

She wanted to comment on the availability of toothbrushes, but suddenly it just seemed like a symbol of all that was different between them.

Who kept a dozen brand-new toothbrushes in the event of unexpected guests, after all?

Exactly the kind of man who lived in a space like this. The kind of man who had nurses touching his arm on the basis of a few seconds acquaintance.

"You must be done in, too." There was something faintly cold in his voice when he said, "I'll show you the other guest room."

And she could understand that completely. She had just hijacked the man's life. Those spare toothbrushes weren't for stray little boys, after all.

She had just shown him he didn't have to be alone with it all.

He needed some distance from that, and so did she.

"Thank you," she murmured. And she didn't just mean for the room. No, she meant for letting her look after Tucker.

For letting her have her opportunity to play auntie before all the evidence was in. Though in her heart, she felt she already knew the truth.

Rory listened to Grace's bedroom door close and felt as if he had been holding his breath and now it was safe to breathe.

Grace in his space.

When he had seen her coming out of Tucker's room, he had turned and looked at her, and known how easy it would be to take it a step further.

Known that she wanted to.

The hunger in her eyes had almost slain his strength.

But it was just wrong.

She was exhausted emotionally and physically. He couldn't take advantage of that.

Plus, Gracie was not the kind of woman he had become accustomed to, not at all. Those women were sophisticated and fast, they had no use for attachments anymore than he did.

When you took things a step further with a woman like Grace?

You better think things all the way through, starting with this thing: she was a forever kind of girl.

The kind that you waited for at the end of an aisle prepared to vow your whole life for her. The kind who harbored dreams of white picket fences and cottages on the lake and children squealing with delight.

And if you weren't prepared to provide a life like that you weren't worthy of her.

And added to that? She was Graham's kid sister. There would be a special place in hell for the man who took advantage of the look he'd seen on her face tonight.

Rory stood by the window until the last of the sounds had died, water running, bed creaking slightly as she got into it.

He let his mind stray. What was she wearing? Her clothes? Nothing at all? One of the old shirts he hung in that closet?

He made himself stop.

They had already waltzed way too close to the danger zone tonight. And he had something he had to do that would not make him Grace's favorite person when she found out.

On stealthy feet, he moved to the guest wing, to the bathroom that Tucker had used, and that Gracie had just exited moments before.

He looked at two toothbrushes that lay on the counter, side by side, for a long time. It was perfect, really. Better than the soda can, because for the soda-can idea to have worked, he would still have needed something of Graham's, or of a member of Graham's family.

He doubted whether, if Grace knew his intentions, she would have volunteered anything in either of those two categories. She had already told him she wanted Serenity—and not science—to deliver the truth.

And would Grace accept whatever Serenity said as the truth? Without verifying it? Surely not. Surely no one was that naive. But then he remembered the cowboys showing up and her determination to believe in a miracle.

Rory wasn't going to take a chance that she could be that trusting. He wasn't going to do it her way. He wasn't leaving it up to her. She would want to just let things unfold, he on the other hand liked to make things happen. He was going to protect her from herself.

Because opportunities like this did not come at every turn. Two toothbrushes. Both, presumably, would hold the genetic code that would prove or disprove if the two people who had used them were related.

He picked both toothbrushes up by their handles, careful not to touch the bristles, took them to the kitchen and bagged them in separate bags.

It was funny how he felt, a familiar feeling. A soldier who had been given an unsavory assignment, who had no choice but to do his duty.

Still, it felt sneaky, and he knew Grace would not approve of sneakiness in any form, even if it would speed up their arrival at the truth.

But from the shape Serenity had been in tonight, Rory knew something he had protected Grace—and Tucker—from.

It was possible they would need the truth sooner than later.

He looked for his cell phone, remembered he had given it to Tucker.

He went into his den, picked up the landline.

If Bridey had been sleeping, nothing in her tone indicated it.

"I need two things," he said. "And I need them fast.

I need a DNA test, I have the samples here that I need tested. And I need a private detective. To find out everything there is to know about a woman named Serenity Chambers." He gave the birth date and the other information that he had gleaned from Tucker for the hospital admittance desk.

He hesitated and then added softly, "I'm particularly interested in the birth of a child, a boy, seven to eight years ago."

"I'm on it."

"It's not about me," he said.

"That was unnecessary, sir. I already knew it wasn't about you."

"Now how would you know that?"

"You just know things about people after you've been around them for a while. And you are not a man who shirks your responsibilities."

"It could have been an accident," he said, enjoying playing devil's advocate to Bridey's complete loyalty to him.

"Or the kind of man who has those kinds of accidents."

"Thanks, Bridey." But as he hung up the phone it seemed to him if Graham, the most decent of men, could have had that kind of accident, then anyone could. A lot of life was luck or lack of it.

Rory allowed himself to feel his own exhaustion. He went back into the guest bathroom and unwrapped two new toothbrushes and put them side by side on the counter. It seemed unnecessarily sly, but really confirmed he was not quite the man Bridey thought he was.

Or the man Gracie seemed determined to believe he was.

And then he went to his own bedroom and felt the unpleasantness of what he had just done.

But despite the fact he had left war zones behind him, despite the fact his bedroom was one designed for a king, Rory had never been more aware he was a soldier. He could be counted on to do what needed to be done.

He could be counted on when no one else had the stomach for it.

He thought of that moment when he had just held Grace tonight. After he had told her about his dreams, shared the burden of his tremendous guilt

When his armor had been down, when he had let go of his need to be strong.

And he cursed himself for the longing that pressed against his chest and felt like fifty tons of steel. He thought he wasn't going to sleep at all, knowing Gracie was just down the hall. Knowing he had confessed his weaknesses to her. Knowing there was a little boy here that he had to figure out what to do with.

But in the morning, Rory awoke, refreshed and amazed.

No dreams.

Gracie was already in the kitchen and he tried to steel himself against how he felt about Grace in the morning: tousle-headed and makeup free, she had slept in a man's shirt that she must have found in the guest-room closet.

She was gorgeous as she snooped through his fridge, making herself at home, making that weight on his chest even more impossible to ignore.

A smarter man would be on his way to Australia.

But Tucker's arrival in the kitchen served as a reminder. Rory was in this now, and he was determined to see it through to the finish.

So, he took them for breakfast at a place that kids liked, though Tucker showed nothing but surliness as he gobbled down enough food to feed a small army. And then they went to the hospital.

Serenity, to everyone's relief was sitting up in bed, looking pale and wrung-out, but as though she would survive. She wanted out, but the doctor would not release her.

Tucker's whole demeanor changed after they had seen his mom. He insisted they drive out to the ponies so he could check on them. Slim was there.

"You know, Tucker," Slim said, "I have a whole pasture out at my place that needs eating down. Why don't I take the ponies out to my place for a while? It would be doing me a favor."

It was put in such a way that Tucker could give in without feeling as if he had absconded on the responsibility he took very seriously.

"I guess that would be good," he said with dignity that was way too grave for a seven-year-old.

Grace must have noticed that, too. As they watched the ponies being hauled away in Serenity's old trailer she looked around the camp with troubled eyes.

But she didn't let on she was troubled to Tucker.

"Want to spend the day with us?" she asked him.

Us.

"I guess," Tucker said, without any real enthusiasm.

"What would your perfect day be?" she asked him.

Tucker looked annoyed by the question. But then, reluctantly, he said, "Never having to go to school. That would be a perfect day."

"Well, it's summer so you already have that. If you could do anything you wanted, Tucker, what would it be?"

His look of annoyance deepened, but then he sighed, and seemed to give in to the frivolous temptation to dream a little.

"My perfect day," he said, "would be riding a horse up into the mountains. I'd set up a camp by a lake. I'd cook hot dogs and have as many as I wanted. Probably six or seven of them at least. And I'd have six sacks of potato chips all to myself. I'd drink a whole gallon of hot chocolate."

He looked like he wanted to stop, maybe even tried to stop, but the dream had taken hold of him. "I'd go to sleep lying right under the stars and I'd feel really full, like I couldn't eat another bite. Not even one more potato chip. I'd listen to the horses grazing, and the water moving and maybe a screech owl.

"I'd be with people who loved me more than anything else. I'd be away from problems. It would be a place where I never worried about anything, ever. And I'd feel safe, like nothing bad could ever happen."

He shut up suddenly, eyed them defiantly, clearly believing he'd revealed way too much of himself.

Rory slid Grace a glance. He could see tears in her eyes.

And he could feel the lump in his own throat. What kind of seven-year-old boy had dreams like this?

Didn't they dream of acquiring the newest toy? If they were offered a perfect day didn't they want to go play with their friends at the swimming pool? Or spend a day at the amusement park? Or go to hockey camp? Meet a sports hero? Or a rock star?

What kind of seven-year-old boy's best dream was being out in the middle of nowhere with a full tummy and feeling safe?

Rory Adams knew exactly what kind of seven-year-old boy dreamed those kind of dreams.

He met Gracie's eyes over Tucker's head. There was that look again, asking him—no, expecting him—to be some kind of hero. He had to walk away from this thing: from her and from this kid before what was left of his heart felt as if it had been ravaged by wolves.

But running away from what scared him most?

That had never been in his nature.

And running away was not even close to the vow he had made to see things through to the end.

He took a deep breath, recognized the irony of both surrendering and preparing for battle.

"Have you ever driven a Ferrari?" he asked Tucker.

CHAPTER EIGHT

IT WAS called Automotion, and it was a go-cart track Grace had driven by a thousand times without giving it a thought.

Now, choosing her go-cart, she wondered what she had been missing all her life. They had a huge selection of all the great high-performance cars in miniature.

Grace watched as Tucker and Rory debated the features of each car as if it were real before they decided which one to drive.

She wasn't just falling for Rory anymore.

No, she had seen on his face the exact moment when he had decided to give Tucker a normal little boy's dream of a perfect day. She had seen on his face the exact moment he had decided to give himself over to this: a sense of being a family.

And she had gone from falling to the ugly part: *splat.*

Splat. As in Gracie Day loved Rory Adams. *Splat.* As in she couldn't stop herself. *Splat.* As in it could have all kinds of messy consequences. *Splat.* As in there was every chance this would not end well. *Splat.* As in Rory would no more reciprocate these feelings than he had when she was fourteen.

Grace had always had a gift for exactly this: seeing

all the things that could go wrong, seeing the potential for disaster everywhere. It was part of what made her such a good event planner. While her customers were doing nothing but having fun she was anticipating every single thing that could go wrong and putting out fires before they roared to life.

So she was astonished to find that after careful evaluation of all the things that could and probably would go wrong as a result of her very foolishly giving over her heart to Rory, she simply didn't care.

She liked the way she felt right now, sliding behind the wheel of her miniature Ferrari.

Alive.

Aware that if you let go of control a little bit, life had crazy potential to go in directions you never expected, and that that wasn't necessarily a bad thing.

She was awake, and being awake made her realize that she had the potential to feel and experience things that she never ever would if she was too cautious.

So Grace vowed she wasn't going to be cautious. She wasn't going to weigh every possibility and every option. She wasn't going to squint toward the future with fearful eyes.

No, she was going to be alive, aware and awake to her own life.

No, she was going to accept with open arms and an open heart the unexpected gift this day had given her. She was going to acknowledge the unexpected gifts she had been given since the day those ponies had broken free and ransacked Pondview.

Wasn't that one of the strangest things about life?

Sometimes the greatest gifts were going to come as a result of an event that you had originally judged as bad.

The Ferrari she chose was yellow and not red. Now she was at the starting line. The track was packed, at least eight little cars were revving beside her.

The pistol went off.

Rory and Tucker took off like they had been shot out of cannons.

It took Grace a little longer to get the hang of it. It was hard to lose that cautious habit, and this activity seemed decidedly dangerous once she was actually moving. People were racing around the figure-eight-shaped track with reckless abandon!

They had lapped her twice when she saw Rory glance back at her, faintly mocking, faintly challenging.

She couldn't have possibly heard him over the roar of the engines. But she must have read his lips.

Let loose, Gracie.

And then, she did. She let go of her need for absolute control. Hadn't the universe been showing her for days that its plan for her was so much better than anything she could plan for herself?

She let go. She pressed down on the accelerator and surged forward. She loved the feeling of power. She pressed down a little harder.

After the final lap, she was still dead last, she couldn't make up for the lost time—and maybe that was another lesson in life. You could not make up for the lost time.

But as she got out of that car, she felt tingly with excitement.

"That was fun!" she said with amazement.

"Tucker and I are going to go again. How about you?"

She looked at the two guys watching her and felt her heart swell. Just like some sort of surrender had happened to her, so had one happened to Rory.

Right now he was the carefree boy he had never been. Even when her brother had brought him home, he might have seemed careless and carefree, but he hadn't been, not totally. Something in him never quite letting go. Something in him watchful and a bit wary even as he had teased her to distraction. Of course, she hadn't seen that at the time. She'd been fourteen! All she had seen was how handsome he was.

And the truth was he was still handsome enough to rattle her world.

She shifted her focus to Tucker. He was shining with happiness.

"Are you coming again?" Rory asked, already heading over to select his second car.

Despite having managed to overcome her cautious nature, she had to acknowledge, secretly, she had been happy when it was over. Secretly, she had felt overjoyed to have survived her own recklessness.

Which meant she hadn't quite learned the lesson yet!

"Of course I'm coming again," she said.

She chose the Ferrari again. Who could resist? And she relaxed a little more this time. Let loose a little more. Came in third instead of dead last.

But what she loved most was watching them, Tucker and Rory, fiercely competitive, both giving themselves over, both learning to play.

Grace knew Rory had probably never had anything approaching a childhood. Not as she thought of childhood.

And so, as with most gifts, as he gave this one to Tucker he received it himself.

"I'm starving," Rory said when they had finally exhausted themselves. She had given up after the third race, but they both had tried every car on the track.

"Me, too," Tucker said approvingly.

"Wanna eat hot dogs till we puke?"

"Yes," Tucker said with soft reverence. "But first we need to go see my mom."

"Absolutely," Rory said, throwing his arm around the boy's scrawny shoulders. Tucker didn't even flinch away.

Serenity was sitting up when they arrived, cursing out a nurse and telling her she'd leave if she wanted to.

But she stopped as soon as they came into the room. Stopped and stared, first at Tucker, then at Rory, then at Grace and then back at Tucker.

And suddenly her fight was gone. There was something in her face that was about the saddest thing Grace had ever seen. Serenity pulled the blanket back over her skinny legs, and said to the nurse. "Okay, then, run your damned tests. But I'm not paying for them."

Tucker scooted up on the bed. "Mama, guess what I did?"

"What did you do, Yucky?"

"Drove a race car!"

She smiled, but Grace could see she was exhausted and that her genuine happiness for Tucker's happiness was mixed with something else. "Fun, huh?"

"The most fun ever," Tucker said.

"Well, they're gonna keep your mama here for a while. I don't want you to worry. I'm tough as an old mama grizzly bear and harder to kill."

"You don't have to worry, either. Slim is taking the ponies to his pasture."

"Slim, huh?" Again, there was some expression, deep in her eyes, that Grace could not completely understand. "You go have fun. I'll be back to my rootin-tootin' self in a couple of days. Enjoy your auntie."

"My auntie?" Tucker said.

"Pretty sure that lady right there is your daddy's sister."

Tucker turned and eyed Grace; she saw that dislike again, naked in his face. Or maybe it wasn't dislike. Fear. Why would he be afraid of her? Why would he be afraid that she was his auntie?

She glanced at Rory to see how he was taking the news. He looked like thunder.

He obviously wanted to say something, skepticism was stamped on his features. But he looked off for a moment, glanced at Tucker, marshaled himself and then he turned on his heel and left the room.

"I gotta go with him, Mama. We're gonna eat hot dogs till we puke." Tucker stopped and went very still. "Unless you want me to stay. I'll stay right here if you want me to."

"Nope. I already told you. Go have fun with your kin."

Guilt and desire warred on his face. "Can we bring you a hot dog?"

Serenity made a face. "Maybe, later, if you think

of it, smuggle me in a little ice cream cone, the kind dipped in butterscotch."

Grace could clearly see Serenity was not up to eating an ice cream cone, she had given her son a little chore to do for her to relieve his guilt. And it worked.

"Hey, Rory, wait up," he called and darted from the room.

But Grace was not so quick to follow. She sat on the edge of the bed.

"You do think he's Graham's," she said softly.

Serenity closed her eyes. "Oh, yeah. I do."

"But why now? Why tell me now?"

"Why not?" Serenity said, something angry in her tone. She opened her eyes, challenging Grace.

"But why didn't you tell Graham?"

"Do I look like the type of person your brother, Mr. Squeaky Clean, would have been happy to know he had a kid with?"

Grace was silent.

"He probably would have tried to take him away from me if he knew. I'm tired now. Just go away."

The words seemed harsh, but there were tears shining behind Serenity's eyes.

When Grace didn't move, she closed her eyes again. Softer, she said, "Please?"

Grace got up and left the room without another word, aware that even as she was troubled, something was blooming inside her.

Hope.

And love.

Tucker was Graham's baby, and it was like the light flickered back on in her world.

She skipped down the hall to find her nephew and Rory. Rory took one look at her face and his look of displeasure deepened.

But she didn't care.

"This is a moment to celebrate," she told him.

"Don't be so sure, Grace."

"Don't spoil this moment with your cynicism."

He drew in a deep breath, as if she had slapped him across the face. But then he smiled, the smile she had come to recognize as the one that hid what he was really feeling.

"Gracie-Facie, that's what I do. I put out the sunshine in girls like you."

"Well, I'm not a little girl and I don't believe you have power over light and darkness."

He sighed, ran a hand through the thick silk of his hair. "Don't count on that," he muttered.

"I've said before that you are unnecessarily cynical," she said. She was aware they were bickering. This was how badly she had fallen: she *loved* bickering with him.

"I told you there's no such thing."

"Are we going to eat hot dogs?" Tucker demanded.

"I guess we are," Rory said. "I guess we are."

And for some reason, he backed off on his cynicism. He looked at her long and hard, and then at Tucker. "I happen to know where the world's best hot dogs are."

She recognized it as a surrender, even if Rory didn't.

"You do?" Tucker asked, reverent.

"Yeah, I do."

Rory watched Tucker eating hot dogs. The little boy claimed he would eat six, but he was petering out after three.

The kid obviously had not had a decent meal in a long time. And then there was Grace. That little smile hadn't left her face since Serenity had announced she was Tucker's aunt.

So everybody was happy.

Why did happiness make him so deeply suspicious? He had a feeling of waiting for the other shoe to drop.

And the thing was? He didn't believe Serenity. Even after Grace had taken him aside and told him Serenity's reasons for not telling Graham that Tucker was his, Rory had serious reservations.

But he'd have an answer in a few days. He wouldn't have to take Serenity's word for it and that filled him with relief.

It occurred to him, he'd had the perfect opportunity to tell Grace about the DNA test. But he hadn't. He had let that moment pass. Why? Because she believed he would not bring darkness to her world, despite the fact she had been properly warned.

And maybe he wouldn't have to. Maybe that DNA test was going to prove exactly what Serenity had said, and he could relax.

And until then, was there any way of preventing Grace from getting completely attached to that kid?

He doubted it. He was already feeling kind of attached to the spunky little fellow himself.

So, he couldn't prevent her from getting attached, but maybe he had to stay near. Watching. Waiting. Being there when that other shoe dropped.

She had asked him not to spoil everything with his cynicism. Okay, then. He'd do his best to hide how he really felt.

Maybe he'd even give himself permission to enjoy giving that kid a few things that he'd never had before.

But unlike her, he would expect the worst, and he would prepare for that. It was how he'd gone through his whole life. It was what had protected him from the disappointment he could see Grace headed toward at breakneck speed, as if she had her foot down hard on the gas pedal of that little yellow Ferrari.

The truth was he had a million things to do today.

The truth was he was losing a bit of control here. Because he *wanted* to be with them.

"Do you want to go to the beach this afternoon?" he heard himself asking.

"I don't have swim stuff," Tucker said, not enthused.

"We can go out to where you're staying and pick it up," Grace said.

"You don't get it. I don't have that stuff. Swim trunks. A beach towel." This was said with a certain defiant pride.

He saw Grace absorb that. Felt himself absorb it.

"That's easy to fix," Rory said. "Ask Grace."

She actually blushed. Rory found himself hoping that if they went to the beach, she would wear her new bikini again.

A little more of that control felt as if it was slipping away from him.

"I don't know how to swim," Tucker said.

"It's not rocket science," Rory said. Unlike Grace, he could feel the pressure of a time line. Within days they would know the truth. Was that enough time to give this kid a taste of a childhood? Something he could hold inside himself when it all went to hell in a handbasket?

Rory wondered if he was kidding himself.

Was this about Tucker, or was this about him?

Since he was Tucker's age he had yearned for normal things. For a normal family. For a normal Christmas. For a normal dinner around the family table. To go to bed at night and not hear raised voices and things breaking, his mother crying. Not to feel that sense of helplessness as he watched his mother unravel; not to feel that sense that he was failing her every single day. Failing to protect her from his father's temper, from her own impulses, from the life that she seemed so disillusioned with.

All his life, he had fought that yearning just to be normal.

Especially when he had met the Day family. He'd liked hanging with Graham, but he had steadfastly refused the invitations to the cottage, for Christmas dinner, the invitation to experience this thing called home too deeply.

At some level he feared that if he ever got what he wanted most, it would destroy him. It would make him weak instead of strong. It would make him squander his moments chasing after something he couldn't have.

And so he had scorned it instead. Held himself aloof from it. Told himself other men *needed* home, family, but he did not.

Every marital breakup among friends, every Dear John letter, Rory had taken as evidence that he lived in reality.

He had congratulated himself on seeing through the illusion, on walking away from it.

And so Rory Adams was startled to find he had no

strength left to fight this thing. Ever since he had told Grace the truth—that he had failed her brother—and she had refused to see it that way, he had felt this weakness growing in him.

And wasn't that his greatest fear, that love made a man weak instead of strong?

Love. Where had that word come from? The word he had avoided his entire life? That he had rarely spoken, and when he did, only in the most casual of contexts, as in *I love pizza with feta cheese on top of it.*

But the truth was what he was feeling for Grace was a whole lot different than what he felt for a pizza, even with feta cheese on top.

Stand down, soldier, he ordered himself.

But his heart wouldn't listen. His heart was prepared to mutiny.

"You're going too fast," Grace called, gasping. "You have to slow down."

She was breathless with laughter and the effort of pedaling her bike up a huge hill. Now Rory and Tucker were swooshing down the other side, speed demons, both of them.

"Tucker, stop it! You just learned!"

But he was already too far away to hear her, and maybe that was a good thing. The last thing he needed was to have the enjoyment of the moment overshadowed by her sense of caution.

She stopped to catch her breath and to watch them.

She acknowledged it had been the best week of her entire life. She loved being with Tucker. She loved being an auntie. It was as though she had lived for this.

But, of course, it was more than being an auntie to Tucker.

Far more. It was the magic of all of them being together. She had let Beth take over the whole office for the past days. Rory must have done the same. Because they were like a family on holiday.

She had lived in the Okanagan Valley her whole life and she felt as though she had never seen it before. She felt as if the scales had dropped from her eyes.

She lived in a state of discovery as they explored and went on picnics and discovered new beaches.

She must have seen sunsets before, but had she ever felt their warmth shimmering along her skin like a living thing?

In the evenings, after the days jam-packed with sightseeing and the headlong pursuit of fun, Tucker's favorite thing was playing video games at Rory's apartment on a state-of-the-art gaming system.

Even she had to admit it was way more fun than board games. She particularly liked the one where you could virtually go bowling, or golfing or play baseball. The laughter they shared at her ineptitude at each of those sports would live with her forever.

They were managing, two or three times a day, to get to the hospital. After that first butterscotch-dipped cone, they always brought Serenity something, made her part of the circle. They gave Tucker a camera and he took a zillion pictures, would climb onto the bed with his mom and share them all. Once they sneaked the gaming system in, and laughed so hard that a nurse came and banished them for the evening and the machine for good.

But, despite a softening in Serenity, at a deeper level, Grace could feel something haunted her? What was it?

Somehow, they were becoming a family. Not a family that met any kind of definition of family, but a family all the same. Grace and Tucker were still staying at Rory's apartment, living in separate rooms, but still, how could you not feel like a family when you were sharing the same space, eating off the same dishes, arguing about what television show to watch, what game to play, thinking about what surprise to cook up for Serenity that day? They were becoming wonderfully good at dreaming up ways to make her smile.

Even Rory seemed to be overcoming his suspicion of her. It was his idea to bring one of the ponies to the front lawn of the hospital where Serenity could see it from her window. Slim delivered it in a trailer. Tucker stood outside waving and grinning. The pony wore a banner that said, Get Well Soon.

But, as exquisite as each day was, and as much as Grace enjoyed every moment of laughter and discovery and togetherness, there was a moment in each day that she looked forward to like no other.

That was when Tucker fell into bed, exhausted. He would call his mom on the cell phone Rory had lent him, and then fall into a deep, deep sleep.

And then Grace and Rory were alone.

There was always one suspended moment when it was suddenly silent. When they would look at each other as if they were thirsty people drinking cool water.

That moment would pass, but the awareness would continue to sizzle softly between them.

It was there as they decided what music to listen to,

or what drink to share as they sat out on his deck watching night claim the lake.

It was there as they talked, the comfort level between them constantly growing, evolving, becoming. They remembered Graham, now, not with pain, but with affection, and those memories brought them comfort and drew them yet closer together.

Without either of them saying a word, somehow Grace and Rory had become a couple. It had started with his hand resting casually on her shoulder or around her waist on some of their excursions.

Encouraged by his easy familiarity she had started taking his hand in hers.

In the evenings now, they shared the couch, closer and closer, together, legs brushing, shoulders touching.

Finally, they had kissed.

It was an intentional kiss, the sun setting, bathing them both in golden light, her shoulder touching his.

And then he had turned and looked at her.

And moaned low in his throat, a sound of surrender, of almost animal wanting.

He had dropped his head over hers, sought her lips and then her throat and then her eyelids, and then she had drawn him to her lips again, hungry for his taste.

And he had tasted of everything he was: strength and power, masculine self-certainty, confidence.

But underlying that, she had been amazed by the pure sweetness of him. That was the taste that lingered after all the others were gone.

In his kiss, he had revealed finally, holding back nothing, who he really was.

And that was a man so genuinely good it brought tears to her eyes.

It was a kiss that there was no mistaking the intention of. It was not *Thank you for a lovely day.* It was not a casual brush of lips where either of them could go *oops, how did that happen?*

No, it was a kiss that said, *I see you.*

It was a kiss that said, *I know you.*

It was a kiss that said, *My heart and yours have begun to beat together.*

It was a kiss that said, *I loved today. I cannot wait for tomorrow.*

In other words it was a kiss that embraced the future.

But then, as if to deny everything that kiss had just said, he had broken away from her, vaguely troubled.

"Good night, Gracie."

And she had been left on the deck, standing in the dying light, so aware that things were not defined between them. It was as if they had become a couple by default, without a conscious decision.

She was afraid if she asked for a conscious decision, if she did anything to disturb the balance, it would end as quickly and casually as it had started.

Now, watching Rory ride his bike down the hill, his hair tangling in the wind behind him, she felt breathless again. Not from riding her bike but from knowing her own heart.

She loved Rory's easy strength, his laughter, his camaraderie with that little boy. She knew she had to find the courage to tell him the truth. She would tell him soon, waiting for the perfect moment.

She would tell Rory Adams she loved him.

It wasn't the cautious thing to do.

But in the past few days, she had become the girl she always wanted to be. A girl who had carried a picture of a red sports car in her wallet without knowing why.

Now she knew.

The car represented the contradiction that was her: she loved home. She loved family. She loved playing games and canning peaches.

But with Rory, she was becoming more whole, more herself, embracing another side, the side that she had always repressed.

The side that was willing to take the lead. The side that was bold. The side that loved adventure.

The side that made her his equal.

The side of her that made her brave enough to say yes to the greatest risk and the greatest adventure of all.

Falling in love with another person. Deeply and truly. Wanting, always, what was best for them.

Even if that meant consequences to herself.

Even if there was the potential there for pain.

Telling Rory Adams she loved him was going to take more courage than anything she had ever done.

And she felt ready.

And somehow it was love that had made her this courageous and this ready.

And wasn't that exactly what love did? Made you better than what you had been before? Made you better than you had ever imagined you could be.

Was he feeling the same way? The very thought made her insides quake, made her tremble with anxiety.

No, she would not let fear into it. She wouldn't. She would be the girl who had dreamed Ferrari dreams.

She kicked off from the top of the hill, took her hand off the brake and kicked free of the bicycle pedals. She had not a single thought of falling.

CHAPTER NINE

Rory stared down at the envelope in his hands. Grace and Tucker were both fast asleep in his guest bedrooms. It was the last night they would be here together like this, the little makeshift family that he had taken such unexpected and fierce pleasure in.

Once they were gone—Serenity was being released from the hospital in the morning—and things got back to normal, how was he going to be able to stand this apartment? It would be as if the light had gone out of it. Even now, glancing around, he realized the place had become a home.

There was a beach towel tossed over the couch, and a remote-control car wedged underneath the coffee table. There were two pairs of tiny sneakers at the front door, Grace's and Tucker's. There was a bowl of potato chips left out on the counter and a tin of hot chocolate and three mugs in the sink.

There was a clumsily wrapped gift on the table, a new blouse that Tucker had picked out for his mother's homecoming.

It felt as if a family lived here.

And over the past week, isn't that what they'd become? A family.

It was what Rory had longed for his entire life. And avoided at the very same time. Now, it had been thrust upon him.

Rory was aware he should not have let his guard down. He should not have been sucked in so completely.

But that's what love did. It impaired a man's judgment as surely as wine. As he thought back over the last week, it occurred to him, maybe even more than wine.

He thought of everything they had done: driving minicars and having picnics, riding bikes, teaching Tucker to swim. He thought of overcoming his deep suspicion of Serenity to honor Tucker's love and devotion for her.

He thought of the evenings in the apartment playing video games, eating chips, sipping hot chocolate.

And he thought of the best moments of all: when Tucker had gone to bed and he and Grace sat out on the deck, sipping hot chocolate and watching the sun set over the lake.

He thought of last night when he had kissed her so thoroughly it felt as if they had exchanged souls.

He let the shock of that ripple along his spine.

He loved her. He loved Grace Day as much as he had ever loved anyone in his whole life.

And love filled a hole in him that he had tried to outrun his whole life.

The envelope had been delivered earlier, and he had put it aside, not wanting to know what was in there, stealing as many moments of this sense of family as he could. He had wanted to have this last night. Of what?

Being a family.

But he had not gone out on the balcony tonight, and

had not kissed her. He had steeled himself against the longing he saw in her face, and his own.

Taking a deep breath, Rory slid the papers from the envelope.

A few minutes later, he set them down, leaned forward and put his elbows on his knees, covered his eyes with his hands.

That's what hope did. Left you open to being broken like this, like a shattered piece of glass.

He hadn't been part of a family. He'd been part of an elaborate pretense, and he of all people should have known better.

He heard her before he saw her, opened his eyes and gazed at Grace. She was in one of his shirts, her hair tousled, her long legs naked.

He had never seen a woman look so sexy.

So beautiful.

"Rory, what's wrong?" she said. "What time is it?"

"It's late."

"You couldn't sleep? Are you having the dreams again?"

He had not had the dreams all week. He had slept soundly. Now, he realized he had failed all the way around.

He had failed to protect his mother.

He had failed to protect Graham.

And he had failed to protect Gracie, too.

When it should have been him being pragmatic, what had he been doing? Throwing himself into the fantasy she had been creating.

"Grace, he's not Graham's."

"What?"

"Tucker isn't Graham's."

She stood there, sleepy and vulnerable, and looked stunned. "What do you mean? How do you know?"

"He's actually not seven. He's nine." Rory thought of that first meeting with Tucker, asking how old he was, Tucker's hesitation, Serenity's voice coming from under the truck.

Tell the man how old you are.

Tucker was small for his age. They'd accepted without question he was seven.

"Given his age," Rory said, "it goes without saying that the DNA was not a match."

"What DNA?" she asked.

"I collected a sample," he said, and then found he could not fudge the truth. Hadn't he been doing that all week? Pretending? Pretending it could all be true. It was enough now. "I collected a sample from each of you."

"Without telling me?" she whispered.

"Grace, you never wanted to know the truth. That's why you didn't want a DNA test from the very beginning. Part of you knew it could end like this and you wanted it all to match your little fantasy."

"I wanted Graham to go on," she said, shrilly.

"Well, he doesn't," Rory said harshly. "Life doesn't always go the way you dream. In fact, it rarely does."

She began to cry.

He got up. He wanted to close his arms around her. He wanted to protect her from the world and from any kind of pain.

But when he began to move toward her, she stepped back from him.

"How could you do this to me? Eventually, I would

have been ready to do a DNA test. How could you collect a sample without telling me? It's a betrayal!"

"I tried to warn you I could put out your light, Grace. I tried to warn you."

She stared at him, then turned on her heel, ran into her room and shut the door firmly.

He stared at the closed door for a moment, and then went to bed. The dreams came back with a vengeance.

At dawn he admitted there would be no more sleep. He got up, a man who had been assigned an unpleasant mission, a man with a job to do.

He went to the hospital.

Serenity was sitting on the edge of her bed, already dressed, ready to go. It would be hours before they released her, but she already was ready. He stood in the doorway for a moment, watching her. He waited for the anger to come at the deceit she had visited on them, on how she had deliberately hurt Grace.

But what he saw in her face in the early morning light was not deceit. It was weariness and fear.

She glanced up and saw him, scanned his face, seemed to sag.

"You know," she said tiredly.

He came and sat beside her. "I took a DNA sample. I put a private detective on it."

"Ah."

"Why would you do this?" he asked. "Why would you cause such a good woman so much pain?"

"In case you haven't figured it out, Sherlock, I'm really sick," she said. She tried for defiance and somehow failed. "I knew before I came in here. I've got Hepatitis C. I'm going to die from it."

He searched her face for the con, and found none.

"I'm sorry," he said. And he was. He was sorry for her, heartbroken for Tucker. But he had to know. "But why visit your troubles on Grace?"

The tears came then.

"In my whole life, one man was decent to me. One. What does that tell you about a life?"

"Graham," he guessed.

"Those few days we were all together. It was a crazy party. He could have done anything, but he never even tried. He never treated me like a whore. He never showed me anything but kindness and respect I didn't deserve."

Rory felt a pang for his friend.

He'd always been like that. Even over there. Keeping his pockets full of candy for the kids. Everyone treated with love and respect. Everyone.

Suddenly, the missing words, the missing part of his dream when he always woke up slipped into his consciousness, but it was gone before he could capture it.

"I saw his picture in the newspaper," Serenity said. "I hadn't seen him for what, eight years? But there was a whole bunch of pictures of Canadian soldiers who had been killed over there. I'm a tough girl," she said, "but when I saw that picture I cried like a baby.

"I guess I started thinking about it right then. What's going to happen to Tucker when I die? I've been in foster care. I didn't want that for Tucker. I thought what if that decent, decent man had a family?"

"What about Tucker's real father?" Rory asked.

"He wasn't a good person. I was never with him, except for a night or two. He died. He never even knew about Tucker. I don't think he would have even cared."

"So, you were looking for a home for Tucker?"

"He doesn't know how sick I am. I mean, I guess he does, 'cause he's seen me not feeling well lots and lots, but he doesn't know I'm going to die.

"Though he must have suspected something was up, because he didn't take to Grace. Almost like he sensed I was choosing who to leave him with and hated her for it. Instead of me.

"But then that first day you guys had him, and he drove the race car, he came in here and he was shining.

"I've never given him that. I want him to have a shot at life. I want him to have what I never had."

Rory felt his own *want* for those very things claw up his throat. Wasn't this what it was to be human? Wanting a family, a place to belong, a place where you felt safe and loved, as basic a need as eating or having a roof over your head? He felt something in him softening toward Serenity.

"There's no hope on the diagnosis?"

"There's an experimental treatment for it. It's the same way they treat cancer. If the treatment doesn't kill you, it can actually get rid of the Hep C permanently."

"And you aren't a candidate?"

She snorted. "I don't even have health insurance."

"If you had health insurance?"

"It wouldn't matter. I still wouldn't have a place to live. Who would look after Tucker on those days I couldn't move away from the toilet I was so sick?"

"What if those weren't issues, either?"

Something flickered in her face—a moment of

hope—and then she tried to kill it. "You won't get this, 'cause you got pure courage coming out your pores. But, Rory, I ain't got no kind of courage. I can't suffer like that."

"Here's the thing, Serenity. It's not really about you. It's about that little boy. And you can't give up without a fight. You can't. Love won't let you. Love is going to ask you to be stronger than you have ever been, and braver than you have ever been. Not for yourself. If it was for yourself, you couldn't do it. But for him, you can. For Tucker you can."

Serenity eyed him, and then the hope flickered back to life in her eyes. And there was something else there too, a startling kind of knowing.

"Well, look at you," she said. "An expert on love. Who would have ever thunk that?"

"Yeah," he said, "Who would have?"

He left the hospital.

Who would have thought he'd be an expert on love? He remembered the look on Grace's face.

How could you?

He'd known all along he had to protect her. He'd known all along what she would need protecting from most was his cynicism, his darkness, his ability to snuff out her light.

He left the hospital. He felt as if cinder blocks were attached to all his limbs. He fished his cell phone out of his pocket.

"Bridey? I need you to find out everything you can about Hepatitis C treatment programs. I need you to find a place for a woman, a nine-year-old boy and eight ponies to live."

"Is that all, sir?"

"No, then I need you to book me a flight to Australia."

Grace was furious at Rory for three days. She could not think of him without feeling that surge of anger. How dare he go behind her back? How dare he take control like that?

And underneath that: How dare he expose the truth? That she was so vulnerable to her dreams?

In a way, those three days of fury helped her cope with the fact that Tucker was gone, too. And that he was not Graham's.

When Serenity had confessed to her how she had been looking for a home for her son because she was ill, Grace had realized she did not need Tucker to be Graham's to love him.

Serenity had gone to live in one of the little guest houses at Slim McKenzie's ranch. Grace had helped them get settled, and between that and getting caught up at work, especially on planning for Warrior Down, she had been grateful to be so busy.

Still, through all the busyness of her days, a part of her waited. She had thought Rory would call. They had been so close. Their lives had become so interlinked.

She missed him so dreadfully. It felt like a physical ache.

How could he not be missing her in the same way?

When she saw his office number on her caller ID, her heart went into triple-time. But it was not Rory.

It was a woman named Bridey. She needed to start putting together The Perfect Day package for the silent auction at Warrior Down. Mr. Adams had suggested a helicopter ride to the top of Silver Lining Mountain, a table set for two, white linen, a chef.

Grace had had perfect days. Seven of them in a row! That was so far from what she'd had!

But she heard herself saying, "Yes, that's fine."

And then, "Is Rory there? Could I talk to him?"

"Oh. I'm sorry. I thought you must know. Mr. Adams is in Australia supervising a job."

She could ask for a number to reach him at. She could leave a message for him. But somehow, she didn't.

He was pulling away from her.

And if she listened closely, she was pretty sure she could hear the sound of her own heart breaking.

But then, she remembered that night long, long ago, when she had seen Rory standing over his mother, fiercely protective.

And in a flash of light she got it.

He saw himself as a protector. The go-to guy. The one who called the shots. The one who maintained control.

He had told her he carried the burden of feeling he had failed to protect her brother.

And he was probably also feeling as if he had failed to protect her, Grace, from Serenity's lie.

All along, he had tried to warn her that he was dark to her light.

Was he trying to protect her from himself?

And who protected him? Where did he rest? Who was his equal?

I am, she thought.

His time with her had made her more than she had ever been before: stronger, more confident, more able to cut loose. She had become more herself than she had ever been before.

And if she could not use those things: if she could not take the biggest risk of all to rescue Rory from himself, then were all the lessons lost?

Wasn't what he needed to know most—and what she needed to know most—that love triumphed?

That love triumphed over deceit? That love triumphed over weakness? That love triumphed over darkness?

That love triumphed, yes, even over death.

Because, somehow, it was her brother who had brought all these events together. Even though he wasn't here, the bigness of his heart had gone on.

Not to live up to the bigness of her brother's heart would be a disgrace to his legacy. To say no to love would be to scorn everything Graham had stood for.

She was going after Rory. And not as Gracie-Facie, either.

No, it was the girl who dreamed of red Ferraris who would find the boldness needed to rescue Rory Adams.

From the terrifying loneliness of the world he had made for himself. Where he had to be in charge of everything and everybody.

And where, because of the hugeness of the task he had set for himself, he was doomed to failure.

The music swirled around Rory. Lights reflected off the lake, and the laughter filled the soft evening air.

He did not want to be here, even if it was for Warrior Down, and he tugged uncomfortably at the bow tie that seemed too tight. He felt alone in the crowd, disconnected. Of course, he had felt disconnected from the moment he had made the decision to leave Gracie and go to Australia.

Now he fingered the piece of paper in his pocket.

I need you. Please come.

The words had been written on an official invitation to the Warrior Down fundraiser. And Rory could not resist them. Not even to protect himself.

Grace needed him. And he had vowed to her he would be her go-to guy.

He had to separate that vow from what he was feeling.

Ever since he had left and gone to Australia it was as if the hole in his heart had grown a little bigger.

The missing part of the dream had come on his second night in Australia.

Two teenage boys. Something about them. He'd hesitated because they were so young. And then bullets everywhere. Ducking, taking cover. Where was Graham? Out there. Crawling out, pulling him back, cradling him in his arms.

Blood, so much blood.

Graham telling him to check up on Gracie, and then a flicker of movement. Those teenage boys, who were responsible for this, for his friend lying dying, had appeared, trying to slink past where he and Graham were hidden.

And he'd snatched up his rifle and pulled it in tight to his shoulder, seen the boys freeze and fear dawn in their eyes through his rifle sights.

And with whatever strength Graham had had left, he had reached up and yanked the barrel down.

"Don't. Not for me. I want my legacy to be love."

Lowering the rifle, the boys slithering away, his chance at retribution gone even as the light winked out in Graham. Forever.

Rory had wanted to phone her after he had had that dream. Had been desperate to talk to her.

And when the dream had not come back at all, he wanted it even more.

But he fought that wanting.

Now, watching her event unfold gloriously, successful beyond what she could have planned, he was determined not to let Gracie see his weakness. His wanting. But the truth was he was growing increasingly annoyed. Considering the urgency of that note, he had barely seen Grace.

She was flitting around like a beautiful butterfly, in a gown spun from golden gossamer. She looked gorgeous. Hair up. Makeup perfect.

Not like a woman pining for him at all!

In fact, she had given him a tiny kiss on the cheek when he arrived, introduced him to some people and then she'd been gone.

Well, it was her night, and obviously she took being in charge of it very seriously. And what a night it was.

The Warrior Down fundraiser had been a great success, a gala on the edge of the lake. The Perfect Day his company had sponsored had been the second-highest moneymaker at the function.

The first highest?

An idea he had scorned when he had first seen it.

Grace had hatched a plan to have people sponsor vacations for military families: four-day excursions into the mountains on horseback.

Rory had thought, cynic that he was, that no one would go for that. They would want a perfect day for themselves. But to give it to someone else? A stranger? Nothing in it for them?

He hadn't thought that would be a big hit.

But it was. The last time he had looked at the list more than thirty families had been sponsored for the mountain horseback holiday.

And all of this was well and good, but where was Grace?

Except for the occasional little wave from the distance, he had barely seen her.

He was beginning to wonder if this whole thing was a joke. A way of her getting back at him for shattering her hopes and dreams, a way of punishing him for abandoning her and everything she stood for and going to Australia.

A note had been slipped to him by a waiter a few minutes ago.

Wait for me. Trust me.

Sure, but finally, the endless evening was drawing down. The crowds were all gone. Now, even the tables were being packed away. The lawns had grown quiet. The dancing and revelry that had happened here were gone, like night evaporated before the morning.

He stood out on the empty lawn, wondering if he should wait any longer.

And then he heard a splash in the dark water.

"Rory! Come in. It's gorgeous."

He squinted out at the water. He would know that voice anywhere. It was too dark to tell.

Was she skinny-dipping?

He cast a look over his shoulder. Sheesh. Anyone could see her.

"Grace, get out of that water. No, don't."

"You come in."

"You're being crazy."

"I know. Quite a departure for an old stick-in-the-mud like me, but you have no one but yourself to blame."

He walked down to the water's edge. She was swimming toward the float. He tugged off the tie, the suit jacket, the shirt, the pants. He left his skivvies on.

"Oh," she called, taunting. "Shy!"

He dived into the water, caught up with her in a few strokes.

"What the hell are you doing?" he asked. He couldn't see through the dark water. Was she naked?

"I'm drowning," she said. "I need you to save me."

"Stop it. You swim like a damned fish."

"I'm drowning in loneliness. I'm drowning in need. I'm drowning in my love for you."

"Gracie—

"No," she said fiercely. "Enough of you being in charge. Enough of you thinking you have to run the whole world. Enough of you thinking you need to protect me. Enough. Come home, Rory. Come home to me."

He stared at her.

"Do you have anything on?"

"Not a stitch," she said without an ounce of shame.

And then he laughed. This was the Gracie he had come to love: spontaneous, willing to embrace the adventure, bold.

This was the girl who had carried a picture of a bright red sports car in her wallet her whole life.

This was her secret side, the side that was for him.

And she was holding it out like a gift, and he could not resist anymore. He could not.

He reached for her, and she came into his arms.

"You have a bathing suit on," he said. He didn't know if he was relieved or disappointed.

"I know. But thinking I didn't got you into the water, didn't it?"

"Diabolical," he said, but gently.

He gave in to the temptation. He pulled her water-silky body close to his. He touched the wetness of her nose with the wetness of his.

"What are you doing?" he whispered.

"I never want you to forget this moment. Not ever. I love you. I want to marry you. I want to have your children. I want to swim naked with you and touch the stars with you.

"I want to be the best I can ever be, and I can't do that without you."

"I'm supposed to ask you to marry me, not the other way around."

"The days of you running the whole world are just over, Rory."

He thought about that. And felt something like relief. Still, he made one last halfhearted effort to show her the error of her ways.

"Grace, you don't know what you're getting into. You really don't."

She took his lips and he found the truth there. She knew exactly what she was getting into. Exactly. She knew him as well as he knew himself, possibly better. She knew his every strength and, even better, she knew his every weakness.

And she was still doing this.

"Actually, I really do," she said. "It might be you who doesn't have a clue what you're getting into."

He laughed and drew her yet closer, nuzzled the curve of her neck with his lips, felt the sensuality of her wet hair on his shoulder.

"You may be right, Gracie-Facie."

"Is that a yes?"

"Oh, yeah, baby, that's the biggest yes of my entire life."

EPILOGUE

Rory lay on his back and watched the stars wink on, one by one in a perfect indigo sky.

A loon called off the lake, that haunting, beautiful sound like no other.

Grace sighed beside him, nestled deeper into the crook of his arm.

A horse nickered softly, another stamped its feet. The bell of the lead mare jangled.

And then the sound of Slim's guitar.

"We should go back," she said. "The campfire is starting."

He twisted slightly, and sure enough sparks were beginning to shoot up behind them as the sky grew darker.

"We will. In a minute," he said.

"This is a good group," Grace said. "Maybe the best yet."

He laughed softly. "You said that last year."

It was the third year they'd been invited to join one of the Mountain Retreat Guest Ranch's excursions for the military families sent by Warrior Down on these adventure camping trips far, far from everything. This year, the schedule was so packed there were hardly enough days of summer. Slim would lead these wilderness adventures, day in and day out, until they could not squeeze one more ounce of time out of summer.

Serenity's voice rose, pure and true above all the others.

"Maybe it's because this is the first time she's been well enough to come that it feels so perfect," Grace said.

No, perfect would be when there were no more devastating illnesses.

No, perfect would be when there was no more war, no more families so in need of this respite from an uncertain world.

But he didn't say that.

Instead he contemplated the miracles around him. Once, he'd been a man who didn't believe in miracles.

But in the face of so much evidence?

Serenity for one. The doctors had not held out much hope for her when she had begun the treatment.

And they had nearly lost her a dozen times in that perilous year. Rory and Grace had been there for her and for Tucker, growing closer and closer, a family of the heart. When his mother was ill, Tucker lived with them, moving seamlessly between their houses.

And to Serenity's credit, she had dug deep and she had never given up. Rory had redefined courage when he had seen her Herculean struggle.

And somehow, through that terrible year of hardship, the real Serenity had emerged. Not hard. Not wild. Sensitive. Sweet.

Slim had fallen madly in love with her, but for the longest time she would have none of it.

Not because her health offered no guarantees, but because she couldn't believe a guy that squeaky clean, as she called him, wouldn't get tired of her.

Her extraordinary efforts to get rid of her suitor reminded Rory of him and Grace at the beginning.

Just like him, Serenity had not really believed that she deserved love.

And just like Grace, Slim had refused to let her believe it.

And so Slim and Serenity had married last year in a simple ceremony with just a few people and a whole lot of horses.

Tucker came now, out of the darkness, sighed with relief when he found them. He was twelve, stretching up the way twelve-year-olds do.

Tucker was not a normal twelve-year-old and Rory had come to understand he never would be.

He was a serious kid, always worried. He monitored his mother's wellness program with the tenacity and fierce devotion of a pit bull.

Now, he settled down on the ground beside Grace.

"Auntie, are you all right?"

Auntie.

Grace had wanted so desperately for her brother to go on. The funny thing was, that he had.

Even though this boy was no relation to them, Graham went on.

In Grace. In Rory. In every single person he had ever touched. In a tiny chance encounter with Serenity years ago, Graham went on. Who could look at this, all of them together, the stars in the night sky, Serenity's voice soaring higher than the stars, and not be convinced of the existence of miracles?

"I'm fine, Tucker, honey."

Out of the corner of his eye Rory saw her reach out and give Tucker's hand a quick hard squeeze.

"What if the baby comes tonight?" Tucker asked, not reassured.

She didn't tell him not to be silly, or that the baby was still more than a month away.

"Uncle Rory has his satellite phone set on speed dial for the helicopter."

Rory could sense the tension ease from those skinny shoulders.

"Remember, a long time ago when you asked me about a perfect day?" Tucker said.

"I remember."

"Who knew it could be better?"

Rory smiled to himself. It was true these mountain days were pure delight and the nights were so intensely beautiful your soul stood still.

But perfect?

Rory's perfect Day was lying beside him and, much as he enjoyed things like this, he had no sense of needing them.

No, perfect was glancing up from the newspaper to see her curled up in a chair engrossed in a book. Perfect was when she made a small fist with her hand and smacked his shoulder with mock annoyance. Perfect was her breathing beside him at night.

Perfect was that moment, nearly three years ago, when she had looked at him with shining eyes and said, "I do."

Perfect was this woman as his wife.

And now a baby, not completing their circle, expanding it.

That secret longing he had always had to belong to something, to find a purpose larger than himself had been found.

Once he had served war.

Now, he served love.

They could hear voices now, raised in song. The songs would begin like this; fast and rowdy, but as the evening grew chillier, the songs would grow more quiet, softer, slower.

Serenity's voice rose up above all the others: pure, perfect and impossibly angelic.

Rory turned his head slightly so that he could see Gracie's gorgeous profile silhouetted by the night.

Just as he had known she would be, Grace was crying, the tears trickling down her cheeks.

And he understood perfectly. He had long ago told her about the end of the dream that did not haunt him anymore.

This was Graham's legacy. Tucker was not his flesh and blood, but this was how he went on, nonetheless. What he had wanted more than anything had come true.

He had asked that his legacy be love.

And against all odds, it was exactly that.

Graham went on in the love.

Rory had a thought, reassuring to a man who had long since realized his power only went so far. He took Grace's hand more firmly.

And this is what he thought: *This is how we all go on, long after the light is extinguished, long after the last breath is drawn. In the love.*

* * * * *

Mills & Boon® Hardback

June 2012

ROMANCE

HISTORICAL

MEDICAL

Mills & Boon® Large Print
June 2012

ROMANCE

An Offer She Can't Refuse	Emma Darcy
An Indecent Proposition	Carol Marinelli
A Night of Living Dangerously	Jennie Lucas
A Devilishly Dark Deal	Maggie Cox
The Cop, the Puppy and Me	Cara Colter
Back in the Soldier's Arms	Soraya Lane
Miss Prim and the Billionaire	Lucy Gordon
Dancing with Danger	Fiona Harper

HISTORICAL

The Disappearing Duchess	Anne Herries
Improper Miss Darling	Gail Whitiker
Beauty and the Scarred Hero	Emily May
Butterfly Swords	Jeannie Lin

MEDICAL

New Doc in Town	Meredith Webber
Orphan Under the Christmas Tree	Meredith Webber
The Night Before Christmas	Alison Roberts
Once a Good Girl...	Wendy S. Marcus
Surgeon in a Wedding Dress	Sue MacKay
The Boy Who Made Them Love Again	Scarlet Wilson

0512 GEN STD LP

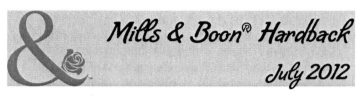

ROMANCE

The Secrets She Carried	Lynne Graham
To Love, Honour and Betray	Jennie Lucas
Heart of a Desert Warrior	Lucy Monroe
Unnoticed and Untouched	Lynn Raye Harris
A Royal World Apart	Maisey Yates
Distracted by her Virtue	Maggie Cox
The Count's Prize	Christina Hollis
The Tarnished Jewel of Jazaar	Susanna Carr
Keeping Her Up All Night	Anna Cleary
The Rules of Engagement	Ally Blake
Argentinian in the Outback	Margaret Way
The Sheriff's Doorstep Baby	Teresa Carpenter
The Sheikh's Jewel	Melissa James
The Rebel Rancher	Donna Alward
Always the Best Man	Fiona Harper
How the Playboy Got Serious	Shirley Jump
Sydney Harbour Hospital: Marco's Temptation	Fiona McArthur
Dr Tall, Dark...and Dangerous?	Lynne Marshall

MEDICAL

The Legendary Playboy Surgeon	Alison Roberts
Falling for Her Impossible Boss	Alison Roberts
Letting Go With Dr Rodriguez	Fiona Lowe
Waking Up With His Runaway Bride	Louisa George

0612 GEN STD HB

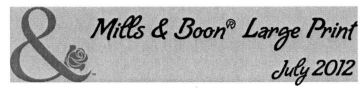

Mills & Boon® Large Print

July 2012

ROMANCE

Roccanti's Marriage Revenge — Lynne Graham
The Devil and Miss Jones — Kate Walker
Sheikh Without a Heart — Sandra Marton
Savas's Wildcat — Anne McAllister
A Bride for the Island Prince — Rebecca Winters
The Nanny and the Boss's Twins — Barbara McMahon
Once a Cowboy... — Patricia Thayer
When Chocolate Is Not Enough... — Nina Harrington

HISTORICAL

The Mysterious Lord Marlowe — Anne Herries
Marrying the Royal Marine — Carla Kelly
A Most Unladylike Adventure — Elizabeth Beacon
Seduced by Her Highland Warrior — Michelle Willingham

MEDICAL

The Boss She Can't Resist — Lucy Clark
Heart Surgeon, Hero...Husband? — Susan Carlisle
Dr Langley: Protector or Playboy? — Joanna Neil
Daredevil and Dr Kate — Leah Martyn
Spring Proposal in Swallowbrook — Abigail Gordon
Doctor's Guide to Dating in the Jungle — Tina Beckett

0612 GEN STD LP